Thirteen Nights of Luck
by
Lacey Dancer

PAPERBACK ISBN: 9798986645445

eBOOK ISBN: 9798986645452

LIBRARY OF CONGRESS: 2022917495

Independently Published by Sydney Clary a.k.a Lacey Dancer

Enhanced and Revised Version

Originally Published under the title 13 Days of Luck (1991)

Cover artwork by Jolene MacFadden

Table of Contents

Letter from Lacey

Welcome to the World according to Pippa and her family and friends. As indicated on the cover, this book is an enhanced reprint. The original title was Thirteen Days of Luck.

Pippa is one of my favorite characters, both then and now. Years have passed since I first met her in my imagination. She broke every rule of category romance that existed in New York at the time. Women were not leads in romance books when the "over forty". Women might have refused to consider marriage as the only answer to loving a man.

If I had been a rule follower myself, I wouldn't have finished the first chapter because I knew the companies I published with would not easily swallow Pippa's age. My agent knew it as well. I wrote the books anyway because Pippa just had to have her story told. My agent and I were right. New York loved Pippa as long as I made her younger. Pippa and I agreed, NOT going to happen. My agent sent the three books to a new company with new ideas for the romance market.

Pippa and her family found their home at Meteor.

She was so popular that the first three books were boxed for Christmas with a bonus stand-alone book. My first boxed set, a special treat for any writer!

Her adventures continued in popularity bringing in the McGuires and introducing two other characters over forty. Trend setting Pippa started yet another trend along with addressing a couple of hot topics in the series. I had such fun with Pippa. I hope you enjoy her too. Because of page length restrictions then, I had to leave out a few details.

The advantage of self-publishing now allows me to ignore page length and just write. *Thirteen Nights of Luck* is longer than the original *13 Days of Luck*.

I do enjoy hearing from you, and I answer all comments personally. However, speed is not always my middle name. My characters often pull me so deeply into their world, that I lose track of time. I do surface eventually and catch up with everyone. You will find a list of contacts on the *About the Author* page at the end of the book.

Lacey Dancer

CHAPTER ONE

"Listen, you stubborn characters, I will not tolerate this idiocy," Pippa muttered, the tip of her tongue caught between her teeth. She glared at the words dancing across the monitor.

Where was that emotional high that usually accompanied the ending of a story? Pippa wondered in disgust as she deleted three pages of garbage prose.

Right now, she felt more like murdering her hero than seeing that he got the woman in the end. She mumbled a lurid oath as she deleted eight more pages. It was the worst dialogue she had done in her thirty-book, twelve-on-the-bestseller-list history.

"I definitely need a vacation," she added, sitting back in her chair, feeling wrung out by the morning.

Her silver-white hair was a silken fall down her back. When she wrote, she preferred comfort to fashion. Today, the choice had been ultra-brief red shorts and a white crop top that just barely covered the essentials. The outfit also showed off a cleavage that turned grown men into cavemen and made women devoutly wish the Creator had been so generous with them.

Her forty-two action-packed years sat easily on her shoulders. No lines marred her smooth skin. Nature had been especially generous in the aging process. No artificial help had been necessary to achieve her sleek lines and elegant curves. She could easily pass for thirty even in unforgiving sunlight.

But none of her physical attributes had anything to do with the real woman. It was a package to Pippa, no more, no less. Had she been ugly she still would have drawn people to her. She was outrageous, with a sense of humor and zest for living that few attain. Her mind was sharp, incisive about others and her work, and extraordinarily single-minded about her wants and needs.

If one ever got past the lure of her figure and looked into her eyes, the pathway to her soul could have been found. The blue depths were clear, bright, and infinite.

Pippa recognized no limits, for she devoutly believed that one could reach the stars simply by putting out a hand. Any problem could be solved with focus and stamina. And boredom was her own damn fault. The latter was the governing source of the moment.

Reaching for the phone, Pippa dialed her travel agent. When her writing was stale, when nothing worked, the answer was always a journey to a new place. She could have handled her travel arrangements via the internet but why bother when she had a friend who excelled in the pesky task of travel arrangements.

"Hello, Miriam, what have you got in trips this week?" she demanded as Miriam answered.

Miriam's face lit up at the sound of Pippa's voice. "Don't tell me you finished that book already," she replied, opening Pippa's file to study the list of places she had already visited. Her client loved to travel and had a grand sense of adventure for the new and different.

"No, I haven't finished," Pippa admitted in exasperation, then laughed ruefully.

"This plot is going to be the death of me...or it. If I don't get out of this house, I'll kill off the characters and they don't deserve it. Besides, the Aretang is doing enough mayhem in this story."

Miriam chuckled, knowing better than to ask what, who, or where Aretang was. Pippa and those unreal but all-too-real space beings were a doorway to confusion to the uninitiated.

"That doesn't sound like the Pippa we all know and love. You never do away with your people unless they deserve it for the story line."

She laughed at the grunt her comment elicited. Frowning, she read over the list of possible packages and discovered little that Pippa hadn't already tried.

"I don't have much right now that you haven't seen."

Pippa grimaced. Nothing of late was going the way it should. Her existence seemed to be filled to overflowing with little hiccups and glitches designed to drive her wild.

Propping her bare feet on the desk, she stared at the landscape outside her window. The view was all too familiar but, this time, lacking in the ability to soothe her mind with its endless expanse of trees and silence.

"Nothing at all?" The feeling of being trapped, confined, intensified.

"Just a trip on the fjords which you've already taken and one to the Grand Canyon, also a repeat."

She scanned the third choice, cataloging the stats. It was unusual enough to appeal to her inquisitive friend. "I do have one cruise that you have missed."

Pippa's feet dropped with a thud, her expression clearing as though touched by a magician's hand. She could feel the prison gates opening.

"I'm desperate. I don't care what it is, the moon, outer Mongolia or wherever, book me on it."

"Pippa, this is a psychic cruise. It's a good one, I'll admit. The main speaker is Joseph Luck. In a world filled with a lot of self styled psychic, he is the real thing. He's helped a lot of people. But this kind of thing isn't for everyone. The cruise is packed with seminars and sessions."

Pippa glanced at the computer desktop. A few keystrokes and she could open the document that had driven her nuts for the last few hours.

Not going to happen. Maybe something as off the wall as a cruise for the paranormal was just the sort of thing she did need to break the spell of boredom that had taken the edge from her writing.

"It sounds right up my alley. I've been reading and writing about the paranormal in my alien sagas for years. Why not get a firsthand look? In fact, I don't know why I haven't thought of it before. You're a genius, Miriam."

Miriam knew that tone. Arguing would be useless with Pip in this mood. "All right, but do me a favor. If you get locked up in some jail or something equally bizarre, don't let your family blame me."

Pippa laughed huskily, her eyes alight with memories. "I promise. Besides, I rather enjoyed my stay at the good city of Rome's expense. You have no idea what one can learn in the lockup. Lock picking, pickpocketing, and quite a number of interesting little sidelines."

Miriam rolled her eyes, thanking every god she knew that Pippa was a friend not family. The idea of watching over her was the stuff of which nightmares were made.

"Pip, so help me, you would drive a saint to alcohol. Woman, you were born to bring trouble into the world. I don't know what I'm worried about. A psychic cruise is just your style.

"Stop maligning me and tell me about this trip."

Pippa leaned forward and propped her elbows on the desk. The fact that the position pressed her breasts together, creating an eye-riveting, centerfold pose never entered her mind.

Even had there been anyone present she wouldn't have noticed. When her attention was caught, mundane factors such as dress and trivial things like eating had no place in her thoughts.

"Well, as I said, Joseph Luck will be the main speaker. He's got a worldwide reputation as a bona fide psychic. This cruise is a bit of nostalgia for him as far as I understand. The other speakers are good, but not quite his equal. There will be public sessions as well as private for the fourteen-day voyage.

You'll be leaving out of Tampa, Florida, on the eighth, and your first port of call will be George Town, Grand Cayman. I'll make up a packet and email it to you with all the pertinent information. There are only a few openings left in first class."

"Fantastic. Book me one. The more windows the better. I may even convince myself to take my laptop with me in case the mood to write strikes."

Miriam chuckled. "All right. If I have to bribe the president of the line, I'll do my best. But just once, Pip, I wish you wouldn't wait until the last minute to call me. This damn thing leaves next week."

Pippa's eyes danced with mischief. "Just in time for my birthday."

"Still on the no-party jag?"

"I love parties, but the morbid thought of celebrating my increase in years is not a good reason for one. I like getting old. Without age I wouldn't have had time to see and do the things I've done. I wouldn't trade that for all the youth in the world. However, I have no intention of sitting through an evening of muted sympathy or forced enjoyment."

"Pippa, only you could describe a party in your honor that way. You know very well you enjoyed the one Alex and Lorelei threw for you last year. If there was any forcing, it was all of us staying way past the time for good night. As far as sympathy is concerned, there isn't a woman in town who doesn't envy you, myself included," Miriam argued bluntly.

Pippa sighed deeply, regretting her outburst. Miriam was a nice woman and a friend, but she was no more able to understand what she meant than her niece, Lorelei, had been.

"I'm just being difficult," she murmured. "You know I'm never nice when a story is kicking up." Because she could almost feel Miriam relax, Pippa forgave herself for the white lie.

"Poor Pip," Miriam drawled teasingly. "Nobody understands you."

Pippa laughed as she knew Miriam expected. "Just you wait. Your fortieth is coming up and you've been divorced now for four years."

Horror chased the amusement from Miriam's face. "Phillippa Weldon. You wouldn't. Just because you fixed up your nephew and your niece there is no reason to turn your matchmaking talents in my direction. I assure you I'm quite happy single."

"Mule whiskers. No one should be alone on a permanent basis."

"This out of the mouth of the woman who makes a religion out of escaping every bachelor's net in the great state of Georgia and probably most of the eastern seaboard."

"That's different."

"Tell me about it," Miriam mumbled in exasperation. "I tell you this. If you do one thing in my direction, I promise you that every birthday you have for the rest of your life will be marked by the largest party my bank account will stand."

"Now that is a threat. All right, I'll behave, but only if you promise to tell me if my relatives get that urge again"

"I'll think about it."

Pippa's eyes narrowed at the evasive tone. "On second thought, I think I'll call Lorelei myself. Talk to you later."

Pippa hung up and dialed Lorelei. "She better not be planning anything," she grumbled to herself as she waited for an answer.

"So far, so good," Lorelei announced in satisfaction, surveying the three other occupants of the study. Diana, looking radiant even in jeans and a yellow pullover sweater, was perched on the arm of the chair in which Jason reclined.

"I can't believe we managed to smuggle you two into town without Pippa hearing about it."

Jason, Lorelei's brother, grinned, his usually cold eyes holding a warmth that had been nurtured by his marriage to the woman sitting so close. He slipped an arm around Diana's waist.

"You don't know that she didn't hear. Maybe she's just planning revenge."

"You don't look upset at the prospect," Alex pointed out, snagging his wife and tugging her gently into his lap.

Jason considered the idea. "I suppose I would be if I lived as near as you two. But since Diana and I have the advantage of the hundreds of miles between Denver and here, I think I can afford a little complacency."

"I think you all are nuts," Diana said dryly, speaking for the first time.

"I agree that Pippa's birthday deserves some recognition, but I don't think this glorified matchmaking bash is going to have any result except every one of us is going to be looking over his or her shoulder for the rest of our natural lives.

If there is an unattached male in any of our circles that hasn't been invited, I don't know his name." Although Diana's tone was serious, her eyes were alive with delight at the situation.

"We invited plenty of women, single ones, too." Jason kissed her neck. "Besides, I'll protect you."

7

"I think that's going to be my line," his spouse murmured, thinking of her insurance policy which even Jason didn't know about.

"It's too late to back out now. The whole town is in on the surprise."

Alex exchanged a look with Jason, both men remembering Pippa's machinations that each had survived to win their women. But, beneath all the planning, there was real love in the room for the woman to whom all four owed so much.

Pippa was and had been a special port in the storm of life for each. Had she asked any of them for anything in their power to give she would have gotten her wish, no questions demanded.

It was because of this love, this debt of caring that none could ignore Pippa's birthday or her lack of someone close to her. Because their marriages had been her gift to each, the same happiness they enjoyed commanded a similar wish for Pippa.

In short, they wanted their favorite aunt to find a man of her own. If, in the process, she stumbled around as they had...well...

The landline rang. Four pairs of eyes stared at it. "It's Pip. I'd know that ring anywhere," Alex said as he picked up the phone and handed it to his wife.

"Coward," Lorelei whispered soundlessly. He grinned and nodded.

"Good afternoon, Pippa," Lorelei said gaily, excitement for Project Pippa shading the husky sound of her voice.

"It can't be afternoon."

"It is. Two o'clock to be precise"

Pippa accepted her niece's word as there wasn't a clock to be seen in the room. Time never mattered when she was eyebrow-deep in the fantasy of her stories.

"I can hear Alex in that response."

Lorelei bent and nipped gently at her husband's ear. "They do say that married people take on the traits of their spouses."

"Not after two whole years they don't."

Lorelei's laugh was a rich ripple of sound as Alex teased her with delicate strokes on her abdomen. Behave, she mouthed silently. His eyes danced with delight and male intent as he shook his head. Keeping her mind on the plan was difficult but she managed-almost.

"You are a grump, aunt of mine. The book not going well?"

"I may never write again," she said darkly. "This monstrosity has been one problem after another. But I fixed it. I'm taking a trip at the end of the week."

Lorelei's sudden change of expression got the attention of her fellow conspirators. "Where is it this time? Siberia?" she asked carefully, striving to appear only mildly interested in the answer.

Pippa was busy trying to decipher the nuances in her niece's voice.

"No. Better. I am taking a Caribbean cruise for fourteen days," Pippa announced, hoping shock would shake Lorelei enough for a hint about the party, if there was one, to slip out.

She described the itinerary and ports of call that Miriam had emailed her.

Lorelei barely heard the description of the trip. Her mind was filled with the logistics of calling over fifty guests and rearranging schedules.

"When are you leaving exactly?"

"Friday. Why? Is there something important going on I should know about?" Pippa asked, deciding a frontal attack was the best line of offense.

Lorelei breathed a silent sigh of relief. Pippa had chosen her departure date on her birthday. It was a good thing Alex had insisted that they hold the party days before to throw her off the scent.

"Nothing special. It's just that I was saying to Alex that you haven't been around for dinner or anything in a couple of weeks. I thought if you didn't have plans tomorrow night you might come over. In fact, I have this new cookbook and I want to try some of the recipes. So, it will be kind of family formal."

Relieved it appeared that she had escaped this year, Pippa was prepared to agree to anything to avoid staring at her irritating computer screen any longer. Besides, it had been a while since she had visited two of her four most favorite people in the world.

"Family formal? I've been looking for an excuse to do some shopping. I don't think I have a family-formal outfit to my name."

"Then you'll come?"

Pippa frowned at the hint of urgency in Lorelei's voice. Suspicion raised its head again.

"This family formal wouldn't have anything to do with my upcoming birthday, would it? I'm going to wring your neck if you're doing something about it after I told you I refuse to count another year. That last party you and your sexy husband had for me was enough to last a lifetime."

Lorelei tried to keep the smile on her face from leaking into her voice. "Now, Pippa, would Alex or I do that to you?"

Pippa tipped her head, thinking. Finally, she had to admit that neither of them would do anything that she asked they not do.

"No," she admitted, then added in a pathetic voice, "Put my disposition down to being a forty-two-year-old old maid."

Lorelei was a too accomplished hand at pure-Pippa theatrics to rise to that bait. "Go enjoy your shopping and let me get back to my kitchen. I want this dinner to work."

Smiling, Pippa ended the call. She had certainly done one of her better deeds when she had helped Alex and Lorelei come together. One taste of matchmaking had hardly been enough. She'd managed to pull off the feat twice when she had managed to get Diana and Jason together.

"Pity, I don't have more nieces and nephews to help down the aisle. It's almost more fun than writing," she murmured as she turned back to the computer. "Who knows, I might even have given Dolly Levi a run for her money."

"She doesn't suspect a thing," Lorelei announced smugly.

Alex dropped a kiss on his wife's shoulder before glancing at his brother-in-law. "It occurs to me, Jason, that it isn't like Pip to obtain a promise from the two of us and forget you and Diana. You don't suppose she's planning some kind of insurance, do you?"

"How could she be?" Jason grinned, the devil dancing in his eyes. He pulled Diana into his lap.

"If Alex is going to insist on an armful of woman while we try to outthink Pippa, I want equal time."

"Your aunt is capable of things none of us has seen yet," Diana inserted, shooting her husband and Alex stern looks.

"It's only fair," her husband pointed out righteously, trying but not succeeding in holding back an expression of anticipation.

"After all, look what she did to us. There was precious little privacy in mine or Alex's courtship. Besides, you know damn well all this talk about getting older is a load of garbage.

Pippa couldn't care less about her chronological age. She's just irritated we put something over on her last year."

He chuckled remembering the lecture he and Alex had received at his eloquent aunt's hands. No amount of soothing on their part had stemmed the flow of Pippa's outrage and frustration that they had been able to outwit her.

The fact that she was fully aware that they had enjoyed hoodwinking her had simply added to the lists of faults she had flung at them.

"I think this bachelor gathering disguised as a surprise birthday party is a stroke of genius." Diana exchanged an eloquent look with Lorelei. She got a shrug and a laugh in return.

"It's a stroke all right. I'm just not sure whose yet."

CHAPTER TWO

The offices of Luck Development Inc. were a landmark in Jacksonville, Florida, a city known for its distinctive buildings. Joshua Luck was the head of the organization in the truest sense of the word.

In spite of being a multimillionaire and having a fully competent staff of people, both at home and in his office, he kept his hand on the tiller of his financial interests. His workday often began before any of his employees even woke up since a good deal of his business spanned a number of time zones, both at home and overseas.

He was known for his precise and expeditious handling of all matters, his acumen in new acquisitions to the increasing family of his businesses, and his workaholic personality.

Four inches over six feet, his height alone made his presence felt when he entered a room. Coal black hair, brown eyes that rarely showed emotion and a face that was a sculpture of sharp lines and planes, he exuded power before he ever spoke a word.

His lean body was more a product of genetics than health club attendance. His voice was deep, a river of authority in which the unwise or dishonest often found it impossible to swim. He had never had a wife, children, or any tie to the world of personal relationships but a brother, Joseph.

If Joshua had all the business flair and drive to succeed, then Joseph had the other extreme. Commerce held no interest for him; rather he preferred the paranormal universe of psychics and extraordinary mental powers. Yet the two brothers had one obvious characteristic in common. Both had well known and respected names in their particular fields.

Despite the extreme differences in their mode of living and beliefs, they had maintained a relationship of sorts over the years. It wasn't a warm, close tie, yet it existed. Increasingly of late, the tentative bonds seemed too flimsy. As the last of their line and the fact that neither looked to be interested in marriage, Joshua regretted the barriers both had accepted and neither had sought to breach.

Today was his forty-eighth birthday. Joshua was in his office as usual, having accepted the congratulations of his secretary and numerous other upper-level management associates. Tonight, he would have dinner with his lady of the moment, Lisa. Perhaps he would even enjoy a little light lovemaking and then he would return home to his own bed.

The order and precision of his life should have pleased him. He had certainly worked long and hard to achieve the even tenor. But the truth was, this birthday was different. He was feeling the effects of his years and, oddly, a strange restlessness that no amount of rationale had succeeded in calming. His thoughts now seemed centered on his lack of a close relationship with Joe.

"Hell, I have no one but Joe. If I die tomorrow, he will get everything I've worked for. He wouldn't understand it. Joe would understand the needs of my people but not how to handle those needs within the framework of the corporate structure. He'll only know the weight of the responsibility he doesn't want," he murmured to himself, an act as uncharacteristic as his familial thoughts.

Memories of the legacy his father had left him, the way Joe had stood against him as he had accepted the weight and the responsibility of the Luck name still rankled as nothing else ever had. Rage twisted within him.

Then just as suddenly as it had come, it died. Joe was not a man who wanted the kind of life he led. He had to accept that. Joe had a right to make his choices. It had taken him years to understand those simple facts.

Joshua had to accept the differences between himself and his brother. He had to let the past lie buried in the ashes of mistakes, hopes, and dreams. Today and tomorrow were all he had. And his brother if he made an effort to reach out, to show him the truths he had come to accept.

He stared out the window of his office, not really seeing the St. John's River flowing far below. For Joshua, thought was father to deed. As always, honesty, professional and personal, was the hallmark of all his dealings.

"For that matter if he died tomorrow, I wouldn't know what to do with his world, either," he admitted to the silent office.

Joshua turned from the window and stared at the phone. Joseph was between psychic speaking engagements. He could call and arrange a meeting. Maybe, if they both worked at it, there was a bridge across their differences.

There had to be. Once they had been strongly bound, true brothers to each other. Now they were barely more than blood related strangers. His decision made, Josh dialed Joseph, waiting impatiently for the phone to be answered.

The room was a quiet haven, the color scheme in soft creams, warm golds, and rich greens a balm for troubled minds and tired spirits. Joseph Luck sprawled in the deep-cushioned chair beside the window.

Sunlight flowed gently through the glass, gilding his skin with gold. His eyes were calm, as smooth as mountain pool that had never known the touch of the disruptive hand of man.

The papers he held contained the itinerary for his latest engagement. He studied the facts, the lists of sessions and the periods of quiet his work demanded. When the phone rang, he picked it up absently.

"Yes, Josh."

"Damn, I wish you wouldn't do that," Josh said, forgetting his good intentions.

Having a brother who could read minds was never something to which he had been able to adjust. He wished he could have blamed Joe's knowledge on caller ID but he knew his brother didn't have a device in his home with that capability.

"Habit," Joe murmured reservedly, for one moment responding as he usually did.

He frowned slightly as he realized there was a new emotion coming from Josh: A tentative acceptance. Joe focused intently, feeling the change as a warm breeze after the frozen heart of winter. A smile touched his lips, growing as the emotion flowed through the phone wire, linking him to the brother he had always admired and loved.

"I'll try to remember not to do it around you," he offered, wise enough not to comment on the change he could feel.

Joshua tensed, then made himself relax. There was no sting in Joe's answer, rather a kind of subtle apology.

"I got the birthday card you sent yesterday. It suddenly dawned on me that I'm getting old." He hadn't meant to put it quite that way but found he didn't wish the words back.

Joe surprised them both with a crack of laughter. "Sure, you are. I read about that failing bank you just bought, an inch ahead of the federal regulators? Bet the thing makes a turn-around in a year or less."

Josh paused, surprised at the references to his accomplishments and business. "I didn't know you knew what I was doing."

"Or cared," Joe added bluntly, finishing the sentence the way it would have been completed even as little as a week ago.

"That, too," Josh admitted without apology. His lips twisted into a wry smile. "It's nice to know I'm not the only one who keeps up. Which brings me to why I called."

"You don't need a reason. Or at least you shouldn't. Neither of us should."

Joshua felt the last of his tension die. For the first time in his life, he was glad that Joe's gift allowed him to understand what most would have needed in words. Gentleness and emotion had never been his strengths.

"You're making this easier than I expected. I don't want to have my own brother living in the same city with me while we do nothing but an obligatory card exchange on holidays and birthdays.

It's not right. We're the last of our line. Neither of us seem to be interested in marriage. The fifteen years between us means one of us will outlive the other. Probably you."

Joe's fingers tightened on the receiver. Josh was offering him the one wish he had always held silent in his mind. He had only wanted a family that accepted his ability and him.

Fear, an emotion strange to him, touched his peace, creating ripples that rarely marred the even tempo of his existence.

"What do you have in mind?"

His cautious question was the result of the pain of the past and the faint hope for the future.

"Have either of us failed at anything we wanted to do?" Josh asked instead.

Joe frowned, startled at the question. "No."

"Then why do we fail with each other? I've been thinking about us for the last few days. The past shouldn't be alive any longer. What was done can't be undone."

He leaned forward in his chair, wishing Joe was in front of him. Depending on his brother's voice alone for a clue to his thinking was risky at the best of times.

Memories filled Joe's mind. Josh and he had been close until their late teens, until the moment when he had realized exactly what his gifts would demand of him. That was the day he had stopped trying to fit into a world that had nothing to offer him.

He had been young, too headstrong to be subtle. He had hurt Josh with his needs and his blatant use of his psychic powers. Instead of trying to build a bridge across the widening river of misunderstanding, he had walked away, leaving Josh with a furious father that neither could love.

"What are you suggesting?"

Josh let out a long breath and with it the tension of facing rejection. "An exchange of information to begin with. I don't understand you or your ways. I've spent years damning your choices.

Now, I want to know. Late decision, I'll grant you, but necessary. I want to see you in action. Maybe I won't like the result any better, but at least I won't make any more decisions based on ignorance."

Joe sat up straighter, intrigued and skeptical, yet hopeful, too. It was more than he deserved for the way he had acted in the past.

"Define what you mean by 'see me in action.'"

Josh chuckled, realizing this was the longest conversation they'd had in years. "Don't you have to go on a cruise to the Caribbean in a few days?"

"How did you know that?"

"Like you, I have always kept up with what you were doing."

"I didn't realize," Joe murmured, stunned. He had been so certain he had killed what little there might have been left from his teenage rebellion and the terrible time after his father's death.

Josh winced at the quiet comment. He had always taken it for granted that Joe knew he cared. As the silence lengthened, Josh tried to think of something to say.

"The only way you'll be able to see me in action is come on the cruise," Joe offered finally.

"I know."

"It's fourteen days of psychic work." Josh had to be really serious to even suggest such a departure from his materialistic way of life. If Josh had ever had a vacation, Joe didn't know about it.

"I know, Joseph. I don't make the suggestion lightly so stop trying to talk me out of it and meet me half way. Or..."

He paused, then added in a rough tone that no one but his brother had ever heard, "...tell me that you don't want to bother being more than a nominal brother."

"No, I don't want that," Joe denied vehemently. "Even when we were kids and you thought I was crazy for my beliefs, you always faced our father down. And the kids at school. Even my teachers. I've never forgotten that."

Josh would have preferred better reasons than gratitude, but he was willing to accept what he could get. "Then let's try. I have a ticket for the cruise, but I'll only use it if you agree."

Joe took a slow breath, reminding himself to accept without expectations. Josh was willing to try to understand what he believed, what he knew was the only way he could live. Maybe this trip would change everything. Equally, it could change nothing. He loved his brother. He had to try.

"All right."

Relieved, Josh started to hang up the phone. Joe's voice stopped him.

"Josh, thanks. You have more courage than I. You always have."

Josh opened his mouth to speak but found himself listening to a dial tone. "Courage, little brother? Not really. Desperation and age can bring wisdom even to a closed mind like mine," he said quietly, replacing the phone gently.

Pippa stared at her reflection, smiling wickedly at the image returning her look for look.

"You are a naughty woman, Phillippa Weldon. It's a good thing this little dinner party is only going to include Alex and Lorelei. Even for you this number is a bit daring."

Daring hardly fit the description of the white iridescent, sheer gown that clung better than a first skin to Pippa's curves. The strapless, backless creation was straight, exquisitely cut to conform to only the most perfect figure.

Scatterings of tiny beads were minute pinpoints of light-catchers in all the right places. Nude silk beneath the thin film of outer fabric was the only concession to modesty, and that was so subtly done that the effect was lost except on the most careful of observers.

"Hollywood fashion has nothing on me," she laughed. "And mine is all natural. No artificial anything."

The rich sound of her humor wrapped around the empty room as she swirled her favorite black velvet, rose-satin-lined opera cape over her shoulders. The drama of the moonlight dress was heightened even more by the Old-World style cloak.

As she skipped lightly down the stairs, she wore an expression of delight for the night that stretched before her. For one moment she wished that Diana and Jason were in town and could share the joy and love of Alex and Lorelei's home.

"This need for family is getting to be a habit," she murmured to herself as she drove the short distance between their houses. "The next thing I know I'll start thinking of husbands and hearths." She shuddered delicately. "I definitely need a vacation."

On the thought, she parked and got out of the car, frowning at the darkened exterior. Odd. Lorelei had forgotten to leave the outside lights on. Not that it mattered. She knew the way blindfolded. Besides, the night was beautiful with just enough of a nip in the air to take the heat from the day. She opened the front door. The house was dark, too.

"Well, I must say this is a nice way to greet a dinner guest," she called, flipping the cloak off her shoulders. "Alex..."

At that moment the lights came on and fifty or more people rose from various hiding places, shrieking..."Surprise!"

Pippa froze. And so did the well-wishers, the majority of whom were unattached males. Had it been anatomically possible, eyeballs would have been pinging all over the floor as the masculine contingency goggled at the sight of Pippa framed in the doorway, wrapped in pearlized wisps.

Jason was the first to break the silence. He dropped an arm over his wife's shoulders and began to chuckle. Alex looked at him, then back at his stupefied guests and followed suit. Diana tried to hold back her laughter. Lorelei lifted her face to the ceiling while rolling her eyes.

"We should have known," she hissed at her husband. She gave him a well-placed elbow in the ribs. "Do something before rigor mortis sets in."

Pippa surveyed the scene, the humor appealing to her. Diana looked amused, Lorelei as though she wished she were in Alaska. Their respective husbands had duplicate expressions of wicked glee on their handsome faces. The rest of the guests had all the mobility of marble statues.

Pippa glanced slowly around, her lips curving in amusement at the scene she had unintentionally created. Her eyes sparkled with sweet revenge as she sauntered toward the closest pair. Retribution was going to be the best present of all on this birthday, she promised herself.

Trust her relatives to find a way around her embargo. "Well, it serves you right, all four of you," she announced, ignoring the eyes faithfully following her every step. She surveyed the enterprising quartet.

"You know, of course, that I will have my revenge. And it will be ever so delicious," she purred.

"Of all the idiotic stunts. This is the second time in as many years that you have gotten past me. There won't be a third."

Not even to herself would she admit that the party filled a rather lonely place in her heart. She slipped her arm into the crook of the closest male, one of Alex's associates from Atlanta, whom she had met and been out with on selected occasions.

"Close your mouth, darling," she whispered devilishly. "I really am fully clothed. You're staring at the marvels of dress-designing genius."

The man, Brad, gulped audibly. "Pip, what I'm staring at has very little to do with fabric," he muttered without thinking; then turned beet red when he realized that not only had the entire room heard him but that he had made the comment at all. He looked to Alex for help, but since his friend was leaning against the wall laughing, there was no aid in that quarter.

Pippa squeezed his arm. "I just love a man who knows how to compliment a woman," she said gently, taking pity on him. She smiled at the rest of the room, including the women, all friends. "I just couldn't resist it. And it was one of a kind."

Diana came forward, her hands outstretched. "On you it's superb." She kissed Pippa's cheek. "It sure put one over on your scheming relatives."

Pippa's pale eyes glittered diabolically. "I wish I could take credit for the planning," she said, eyeing Jason with no nice intent.

"I can see I'm in for it now," he muttered.

"Not from me just yet." She looked Diana over thoroughly. "But I would say in a few months, I'll have my revenge."

Diana blushed faintly as her husband looked first startled, then, as comprehension dawned, shocked.

"Diana Starke, you didn't tell me."

Diana knew that look. Jason rarely got into a temper, even now. But when he did, the walls trembled. She had to say something quick.

"You wouldn't have let me come if I had. Besides, we had that benefit to do." She put on her most winning smile.

Ignoring the smile and the room full of spectators, Jason caught his wife in his arms, shaking her once, gently, before kissing her hard. "Of all the idiotic stunts."

Pippa grinned at their reaction. The evening was providing all sorts of bonuses. "Two down and two to go," she murmured, turning to the other pair of conspirators.

Alex, still chuckling, held up his hand. "I'm not even going to try to be a gentleman and take half the blame. It was not our idea."

"But it is your house."

Lorelei tucked her hand into Alex's. "I'll protect you," she assured him solemnly. "Besides, I'm not pregnant and you know every secret I've got."

Pippa was neither faint hearted, blocked, nor unimaginative. "I was thinking more along the lines of teaching Bouncer a few tricks for his rider's amusement. Things like how to buck on command. Sitting down at a certain signal."

Since Alex's prowess on the surprisingly high-spirited, frequently stubborn black gelding was one of the town's topics of conversation, the guests laughed. With that kind of beginning, the evening could only be a success.

The party went on until four in the morning. By the time the last guest wandered into the predawn light, Pippa had shed her shoes and her hair was swirled about her shoulders, the silvered strands seeming to mesh with the threads of the gown.

"I really did enjoy myself in spite of the fact the party was probably the heaviest-handed attempt at getting me paired off with a man that the world has ever known," Pippa said, curling into the cushions of the couch in front of the living-room fire.

She slowly twirled the last of the wine in her glass before lifting her head. Her eyes were grave, so unlike their usual expression that she caught the full attention of her relatives. She loved them all.

Jason, her nephew, the Olympic champion ice skater with the frozen emotions. His wife and mate Diana Diamond. An ice choreographer so highly sought by any skater intending to shoot for the gold in the highly competitive ice-skating arena.

Lorelei, a world class gymnast on the verge of taking the gold in the Olympics until an auto accident almost destroyed the life she had worked so hard to build. The doctors' verdict, paralysis, no walking ever.

She had proven every doubter wrong. She had fought for every step she took. Alone, until Alex, the entrepreneur with a workaholic lifestyle that was slowly killing him made a place for himself in her life, accepting her limitations and her strengths.

Pippa knew she'd had a hand in each pairing. However, she had been subtle. Certainly, she had never been as heavy handed as her relatives and spouses had been tonight. Their concern had to stop. She loved them for it, but she didn't need their expectations for what her future should hold. She loved her life exactly the way it was. If she hadn't, she would have changed it.

"I wish all of you would stop worrying about me. I really am just as I wish to be. I won't lie to you and say that I am never lonely. I won't tell you that I don't enjoy having men fall over chairs when I walk into the room. I wouldn't be human if I didn't like the effect."

She paused, looking at each separately, loving them all, more than happy they were her family. "I have you and whatever children you bring into the world. I have my freedom and I have acceptance for the woman I am. It is enough."

Diana leaned tiredly against Jason's side, watching the face of the woman she both admired, feared for, and loved. Understanding slipped slowly into her mind. She glanced around, seeing the same realization in the eyes of Jason, Alex, and Lorelei.

Pippa's greatest gift to them had been her acceptance of their differences. She had asked nothing of them but that they be happy. But they had not returned Pippa's gift. Instead, they had sought to change the woman they loved.

Diana rose, going to Pippa, taking her hands. "I love you."

Jason joined his wife, slipping his arm around her waist, giving thanks for the promise of life that was even now growing in her body.

"We all love you, Pip."

Before the warmth of Diana's love in his life, he wouldn't have had the courage to say those words aloud, much less admit to himself he was capable of feeling any emotion beyond his dedication to his skating. Before Diana, Pippa had been the only one who had ever understood, without words all that he was.

"We didn't want you to be alone anymore," Lorelei murmured, wishing her crippled leg would permit the same gesture that Diana had made. The party had tired her more than she wanted the others to know. "We didn't think beyond that."

Pippa, her empty glass in hand, got to her feet. She lightly touched Jason's hand then Diana's cheek. Unaccustomed tears glistened in her eyes. She fought the emotion as she fought anything that reminded her of weakness.

"If we don't stop this conversation right now, someone is going to be sniffling. I hate crying." She moved to the bar to pour herself another glass of wine. "Let's talk about something exciting, like my trip. I half expected someone to try to talk me out of my psychic cruise."

For one moment, silence held sway as her audience tried to adjust to the change of subject. Pippa sipped as she waited for the four to process her plans.

"Psychic cruise? When you said cruise, you didn't specify," Lorelei commented faintly, glancing at the others in the room. She felt marginally better on seeing that they seemed as nonplussed as she felt. "Maybe I'm the only one who doesn't know what that is, but what is it?"

Pippa settled into her place, smiling mysteriously, glad the emotional tide had turned.

"Something like a floating seminar. You do all the usual cruise things, stop at certain ports, shop, sightsee, that sort of thing and, in between, talks are given by the guest speakers. You can even arrange for private readings, fortune telling, psychometry, numerology."

"This is research, right?" Jason said hopefully, having a terrible feeling it was nothing of the kind.

Pippa shook her head, her face calm, her eyes sparkling with mirth and determination. "A whim. I've been housebound for two months. It's time to fly again."

The four exchanged looks, each aware of their new resolution. It was left to Alex, the most diplomatic of the two men, to say, "Should we keep bail money available?"

Laughing, Pippa shrugged. The light caught the beads on her dress, sending seductive messages to an unreceptive audience. "Now, how would I know? I didn't expect to be arrested as an Italian call girl or whatever the term is on that trip. And besides, that was four vacations ago. What can happen on a cruise ship?"

"To you...anything," Jason responded bluntly. "Just remember, Diana is in a delicate condition now. So, you'll have to behave or you might upset your godchild."

Pippa opened her lips to reply before his words sank in. "Godmother. Me? I? Whatever?"

"Who better? Without you, we probably wouldn't be in this situation."

Diana joined Pippa on the couch. Dark eyes met light. "Say you will."

Pippa's smile, without the devil that usually lurked in the pale depths, would have lured the angels from heaven.

"I would love it. For that I will behave." Setting her full glass on the table, she enveloped Diana in a hug. "What are we having? Boy or girl?"

Jason laughed. "Why don't you order for us?"

Pippa looked at Jason over Diana's head. "I think one of each," she suggested, the devil back with a sting.

Alex chuckled. "You led with your chin on that one, Jase," he pointed out as his brother-in-law paled. "When Lorelei gets in this interesting condition, we are going to Siberia until it's over."

"Won't work. She'd probably follow you."

Pippa fixed Alex with a stern look. "He's right I would. And I wouldn't behave on the way."

"Shut up while you're ahead, darling. I don't want my unborn child argued over anyway," Lorelei murmured, tucking her arm in Alex's.

"Pippa, do us all a favor and find a sexy male to keep you occupied while you're away," Alex said, feeling distinctly hunted.

She shook her head. "Not me, my friend. He'd really expect me to behave, and that's like asking the weather to be predictable. We like keeping mankind on its toes."

CHAPTER THREE

Joshua slid out of his Jaguar sedan and walked leisurely around the car to open the door for his companion. Long nylon-clad legs emerged as Lisa unfolded from her seat. Almost as tall as he with the impeccable grooming and bearing of inherited wealth, Lisa Ridgemont had graced his arm and occasionally his bed for the past eighteen months.

Theirs was a careful relationship, for both were careful people. Lisa, despite her money, was a career woman, a lawyer to be precise. And she was precise. Every move she made was planned. Her gestures, her voice, her choices were all restrained, discreet, and totally correct for every situation.

Joshua admired her control, found pleasure if not excitement in her sense of order and decorum. If he occasionally found her actions a bit too predictable, he stifled the errant thought and concentrated on Lisa's many virtues.

"You're very quiet this evening, Joshua," Lisa murmured after she had taken her place across the intimately small restaurant table. "Bad day?"

"Not particularly." He smiled faintly. "I was thinking about Joe."

She raised her brows, for the topic was not one they discussed often or openly. "It must be difficult for you to have a notorious psychic for a brother."

A faint frown of displeasure slipped over Joshua's face. "I'm not sure notorious is the correct word," he said, curbing his irritation at the description. As little as a week ago, he might have let it pass without an emotional ripple. "Renowned or famous would be better."

Shrugging delicately, she tendered an apologetic smile. "My lawyer personality showing through. I'm not good with things I can't hold in my hands."

The subdued lighting highlighted her expertly made-up face. While not beautiful, her features had an aristocratic look that drew the eye and made one wonder what went on behind the calm expression with which she habitually faced the world.

"I'm sensitive on the subject," Josh admitted with a sigh, wondering when this stage or whatever it was would pass. He was tired of being ambushed by his own feelings.

She touched his hand lightly, smiling. "Family have a tendency to make us all touchy, especially if one is a little different. You and I are rule followers, some would even say boring, so I suppose to the more exotic of our relatives we seem stodgy."

Joshua knew she was trying to make him feel better, but her word choices only succeeded in making him feel old, less a man and definitely set in his ways. What he could have laughed off at twenty-eight had more of an impact at forty-eight. He was not in the mood to have warm milk on a tray yet.

"I thought I would go on this next cruise with Joe."

Lisa laughed softly, thinking he was teasing.

"Taking up fortunetelling? You'd have the men standing in line to see what you would tell them about their investments."

Joshua frowned, but before he could say anything the waiter arrived to take their order. By the time the man departed, the mood had changed.

Lisa began a quiet conversation on the ramifications of a corporate case she was handling, and Josh found himself involved in the lengthy exchange that should have held his interest and yet it didn't. When the food arrived, it was delicious as always.

Lisa was the perfect companion, and he was irritable and trying not to show it. No matter what topic of conversation, he discovered that something Lisa said would annoy him to the point that he was biting back a number of sharp comments.

The topper for the evening was when he took her home and realized that she expected him to stay for a while. He had forgotten that had been his intention at the beginning of their date.

"I don't think I would be much of a partner," he said, turning to her in the darkness of the car. Guilt sat uneasily on his shoulders.

Lisa's perfect brows arched. "You mean because you're rather irritable?"

Irritable made him sound like a fractious child, he thought angrily.

"I had hoped you wouldn't notice. I don't know what's bothering me." It would hardly be polite to inform Lisa that her dialogue had all the excitement of a phone book recital.

"Your birthday probably. I remember my thirty-fifth. I had irritability down to an art form."

She touched his hand. When he didn't pull away, she lifted it to her breast. "Sex with you is always pleasant, relaxing. It's been a tough week for me. Maybe we both need to be together."

Stunned at her boldness, for Lisa always waited for him to initiate their lovemaking, Joshua was at a loss. He stared at her, seeing his fingers as dark shadows against the cream of her silk dress. Her body was soft, warm, and her mind was willing.

His was not. Suddenly, pleasant and relaxing seemed criticisms rather than compliments. Was he so old that the fire of passion was no longer possible?

Was he so predictable that wanting was too messy to be acceptable? Was he so accustomed to making love with Lisa that relaxing was the best he could hope for? Every instinct shouted no.

"What about love?"

Lisa frowned, disturbed at the sudden anger in his voice. "Between us? Whatever for? You have your career and life and I have mine. Neither of us wants children or has the time for a full-scale commitment. Look at your travel schedule. Look at my court calendar. Where on earth would we put love?"

As short a time as a day ago, they wouldn't have been having this conversation. Lisa was only saying things that he had believed himself.

"I don't think you put love anywhere. It's just there," he said slowly.

"Not for us, it isn't. Emotions cause more problems than they're worth." She leaned away from his hand.

Joshua let his fingers drop, realizing what he should have seen a long time ago. There was a bloodless and heartless quality to his personal relationships that was shocking. No wonder Joe didn't understand him. For the first time in his life, he didn't understand himself.

"Lisa, I want more than that," he said carefully, watching her, hoping he wasn't hurting her, but not even sure she could be hurt.

"Why?"

A good question, but one to which he had no answer. "I don't know. I just know that this isn't enough. I'm not saying that there is any fault in you. We've always been honest with each other. I won't lie to you now. I want to feel things."

"You do. You care about your business. You have integrity, honesty. You make love perfectly."

That word again. He was beginning to hate it. "Life isn't perfect. It has twists and turns, hills, valleys, lows, highs."

Lisa shook her head. "Don't do this to yourself. I've been through this introspection and it's nothing but a load of hype that accomplishes nothing. We are what we are. No amount of midlife crisis thinking, and well-meant resolutions change patterns of a lifetime."

She gathered her purse. "I care about you, Joshua. When you start acting like yourself, when you stop expecting more out of either of us than we can give, let me know." She got out of the car, closing the door gently behind her before walking away without a backward look.

Joshua started the engine, feeling lighter than he would have thought possible. His irritation was a leaf blown away by the wind. Tomorrow he would board a plane for the short trip to Tampa.

From there he would board the cruise ship for fourteen days. A vacation. A chance to finally find a path to a relationship with his brother. He would also have time alone to think without anything or anyone to interrupt the process. Maybe he would find some answers for the second half of his life.

Lisa had shown him tonight what he had become. She was happy in her secure, well-charted niche. He was not. There had to be more to life than the next deal, the occasional pleasant, relaxing moments in bed, and a quiet talk of nothing important over dinner.

When was the last time he had done anything on impulse? Dared to be different, said what he really thought or tried something new? he wondered as he parked the car in the underground lot of his high-security apartment building.

The ride to the penthouse was swift and solitary. The rooms of his suite were a decorator's dream of a marriage of antique and modern. The colors were vibrant with jewel-like clarity. Everything in his living quarters was placed exactly in the right spot, at the precise angle to display for maximum effect.

In short, perfect. He leaned over slightly, turning a piece of sculpture to a different view. Immediately, he faced the urge to return the art to its original position. He straightened, staring at the change, fighting the need to set the small world to right.

Perfection. I hate the word, he thought to himself. And no, damn it, this thing is staying where it is. Lisa is staying where she is and I'm going to get out of this rut before I get so entrenched that dynamite won't budge me.

There has to be more to life than this. There have to be people in this world, functional people who do things on the spur of the moment, for the sheer joy of it. There has to be a woman, a real woman of my age who knows how to live.

"I will never have relaxing sex again," he promised himself aloud, shaking his head in deep disgust. If it isn't worth passion and wanting, then it damn well isn't worth my time doing.

"This is it," Pippa announced eagerly over the noise of the people rushing about the Atlanta airport terminal. She turned to hug Lorelei, then lifted her face for Alex's good-bye kiss.

"Thanks for driving me into the city and for the send-off dinner with Diana and Jason last night. I'm ready to face two weeks of strange menus now."

"Lorelei needed a break from the country," Alex said, slanting his wife a sexy grin. "And you know very well you're going to love every minute of your trip so don't try your wiles on me. I'm married, remember?"

Lorelei tucked her arm in his, laughing up at him. "Behave. You have everything, don't you?" she asked, turning to Pippa.

She nodded. "Yes, Mommy. I wonder how you think I survived all these years without you to mother me."

She shrugged, the off-the-shoulder-blouse she invariably favored sliding down her arm. In her white designer jeans, with her hair pulled up in a colorful clip and her bright-eyed anticipation, she made a mockery of her age, a fact noticed by more than one appreciative male.

Lorelei shook her head. "I promise I'll do better next time."

Pippa kissed her cheek. "No, you won't. I quite like having someone chasing after me."

"Liar," Lorelei scoffed good-naturedly. She knew very well Pippa allowed her scolding for her sake rather than Pippa's own.

Pippa grinned as she hefted a large tote bag over her shoulder, hiked up the edge of her blouse, and looked toward boarding gate. The line of people was down to the last few. "It's time for me to take off."

Leaning her head against Alex's shoulder, Lorelei smiled at her barely restrained impatience. "Scat, Pip. Before we decide to keep you here."

"Take care you don't come back with the entire male population of the islands in tow," Alex teased.

Pippa's flashing smile touched them both. "The thought had never occurred," she replied huskily as she sauntered away.

"She worries me in that devil-may-care mood," Lorelei murmured, watching Pippa walk through the gate with two men following in her wake. Her seductive walk and knockout figure made her a vivid ray of life in the jaded throng of travelers.

"You forget that beneath that siren's body is a woman with more courage and brains than ten people. If she has ever backed away from a problem or a challenge, I've never seen it. She'll always fly higher and faster than the rest of us. That's her nature."

"But she's always alone. Since I found you, I realize what that means. I always used to think that Pip could handle anything. But what if someone hurts her? Just thinking about it makes me so angry that I think I would want his heart on a platter."

Alex leaned forward and kissed his bloodthirsty mate. "You'd have to stand in line with Jason, Diana, and me, love of my life. And that's assuming Pippa didn't hand out her own form of retribution. Now stop worrying. Pippa knows herself well. She isn't meek and she isn't naive. Frankly, I don't know a man for whom she isn't more than a match."

Pippa eyed her ticket and the numbers on the seat. The bag on her shoulder was heavy but not something she had wanted to check with her luggage. She could handle being without clothes but not without her notebook and laptop.

One never knew when an idea would strike, she thought as she tugged the bag away from the edge of one of the cushions along the aisle. Finally, she found her seat and settled in with a sigh. For the moments left of boarding she studied her fellow first class passengers, disappointed when she found no one who presented new characteristics in her never-ending search for human material for her books.

Leaning back, she loosened her hair clip and pulled out a current paperback. Flying was her least favorite thing in the world. If she couldn't divert her mind with character sketches, then reading was the only alternative.

Besides, the plane had a stop in Jacksonville. With luck there might be something worth looking at in the new batch of passengers that would be boarding. Otherwise, what was actually a short flight was going to be very long indeed.

Pippa was so deep into the historical story she was reading that she hardly noticed when the plane touched down for its one and only stop on the route. She didn't look up as some of the people got off, and only occasionally as a few got on.

Suddenly, the most delicious masculine fragrance caught her attention. She raised her head, her nose following the scent to the man who had just passed. She could only see his back, the broad shoulders, narrow hips, and the most majestic walk that she had ever encountered. The man moved as though the space around him was unlimited, the noise level nonexistent and the world his own.

It was not arrogance, rather a regal quality that was at once eye-riveting and rare. She had to see his face. Craning her neck, she watched as he sat down. But not once did he turn his head from full forward nor did he appear interested in the routine of preflight instructions.

Intrigued, curious, artistically, of course, Pippa fidgeted in her seat, angling for a better look. None came. When the plane was in the air and the seat belt sign off, she could stand the suspense no longer. She had to see his face, to know if it matched the uniqueness of the rest of him.

Deciding a turn up the aisle would get her a look, she rose, stretching idly, missing the pop-eyed expression of the man beside her who had spent the first ten minutes of flight trying to engage her in conversation.

She sauntered toward the front of the first-class section, turned and walked back. Damn, she thought. He had his eyes on the papers in his briefcase so all she could see was a heavy pelt of black hair, so dense that she ached to slide her fingers through the inky strands. Without realizing it, more curious than ever, she bent slightly, her walk slowing. That she had the attention of quite a few of the male passengers bothered her not at all.

Suddenly, almost as though she had willed it, the man looked up, his brows raised. Pippa found herself staring into the most expressionless dark eyes she had ever seen. Startled, she stopped, trading looks with interest. His face was all she could have hoped for and more.

This was MAN in capital letters. He had seen the world or what he wanted of it and had come away unimpressed. He walked alone out of choice, and he took no prisoners. The phrases popped with the speed of hyperdrive into hyper consciousness. None could be denied.

"Do you always stare at strangers?"

The voice was as smooth as rare brandy and had the same well-disguised punch.

"Only when they interest me as much as you do." she replied honestly.

There was a vague familiarity about his face that was puzzling. She knew she had never spoken to him before. She would have remembered that voice.

He didn't even blink. "You're blocking traffic."

Pippa looked around, not afraid of breaking eye contact for she knew he would still be there waiting when she turned back. This man turned away from nothing.

"So I am," she agreed, angling her body sideways to allow the flight attendant to pass. She glanced at him, smiling faintly. She didn't expect a similar gesture and wasn't disappointed when he continued to study her.

"Your companion?" She gestured to the older woman sitting beside him.

"No."

Pippa's smile widened as she leaned forward to the woman who had watching the exchange with interest. Restraint had never been her strong suit.

"I wonder if I could ask a favor? I'm a writer, you see. And this man would make the most marvelous hero for my next story. Would you mind very much if we trade seats so that I can interview him? I have a lovely window seat four rows back."

Off guard, startled by Pippa's friendly manner, the woman looked to the man, getting no help. "I read a lot." She gestured to the book in her lap. "Would I know you?" she asked hesitantly.

Pippa put on her most winning expression. "If you read sci-fi you might. J.B. Starr." Pippa rarely traded on her fame unless it was absolutely necessary.

The woman's eyes widened, a delighted grin touching her face. "Really. I love your books." She dug into her tote as she stood. "I even have one of them with me. Would you autograph it?"

"Gladly."

Pippa held out her hand, accepting the book and pen the woman pulled from her oversize purse. She scrawled a message and her signature with a flourish, eager to get to her purpose. The man said nothing. In fact, he paid them no attention as he redirected his glance to his papers.

Pippa walked the woman back to her seat, picked up her own tote, and retraced her steps. The man angled his legs, allowing her to slide by but otherwise ignored her. Pippa curled comfortably into the cushions, extracted her notebook and studied him expectantly.

She had discovered early in her career that most people responded favorably to being in print and almost everyone loved being the focus of genuine interest. The seconds ticked into minutes, and he still didn't look up. Pippa frowned.

"I really meant it, you know," she said finally.

No answer, just the measured flow of pen across paper.

Pippa found his challenge commanded even more of her curiosity. "The flight isn't all that long and I promise I won't take much of your time and it would really mean a lot to me." The last she added in her most beguiling voice.

"I'm not interested in your books," the man said without looking up.

"That's all right. Not everyone is a fan. Lately, I'm not even sure I like them myself. Stubborn characters."

The wry humor caught Josh's attention when nothing else would have. He looked at her. No, she hadn't gotten any less devastating than when she had leaned over him. The blouse was still more of a tease to his senses than a reality, and that face was responsible for the last three errors he had made in his computations.

Beautiful didn't begin to describe her. But physical attributes didn't make up for the fact that the woman had a brazen way of looking at him that was distinctly annoying. Her manner was anything but discreet. He eyed the brief top, damning the shoulder that kept sliding down, giving peek-a-boo glances at more ivory skin than the law should allow. The jeans were just as revealing, snug, trim, and faithful in their tracing of the lush figure they embraced.

Pippa watched him watching her and wondered what he was thinking. That face could hide the secrets of the ages and still look as though it knew nothing. Had he been born that inscrutable or was the trait an acquired one?

"How old are you?"

The unexpected question startled Josh into answering when he would have refused. "Forty-eight. Just."

She smiled. "I know you couldn't be as young as you look. Your control is too finely tuned."

He blinked, frowning, at the odd compliment and her perception. Not for a second did he believe that bit about her being a writer. The woman was just an accomplished liar.

"Should I say thank you?"

"For the truth, hardly." Pippa shrugged, the blouse, in accordance with the laws of gravity sliding farther down her arm.

Josh watched the slow show of more satin flesh with fascination. The woman was lethal and didn't seem to care at all. She had a voice that reminded him of every fantasy he'd had as a young buck. Her body made him wish he were still that young. The look in her eyes that told him no matter what time did to that beautiful form, nothing would dim the ardor of the owner.

Envy was so subtle he almost missed the influence. He had asked for a woman who was the exact opposite of Lisa. The gods had answered. Now he had a choice. Follow the dictates that had governed his life for so long or accept the gift beside him, enjoying it for the duration of the trip to Tampa.

He stared into her pale eyes, liking the way that she looked straight back at him. Her boldness was, suddenly less irritating. Admiration for her courage and ingenuity seeped in, rearranging his thoughts. What had he to lose? Once they landed, he would never see her again.

"How old are you?" he asked, putting away his papers without looking at them.

Pippa's smile widened. "Forty-two. Just." She glanced at the briefcase. "Are they very important?"

Josh relegated the multimillion-dollar deal to two words. "Not very."

Pippa laughed, settling back to enjoy the unexpected bonus of the flight. "Good. I hate feeling guilty."

"Do you often?"

"No." She grinned wickedly, liking the husky ebb and flow of his voice. His first answers had been clipped, authoritative. "I leave that for the worriers of the world. Now tell me how tall you are."

"Six feet four."

"Brothers?"

"One."

"Same height?"

"Yes."

"Oh, good. I had hoped it was hereditary. Your father, too?"

Josh watched her face, wondering when she was going to get to asking him his name. "Yes."

Suddenly it occurred to him that she might already know it. He didn't kid himself into believing that every woman he met was a gold digger, but this one could be. The designer jeans and the silk blouse were definitely provocative and eye catching.

And unless he was mistaken, which he rarely was, those clear stones in her ears and that rock on her finger were blue-white diamonds. The tote she carried had seen better days, yet her hands were soft, as though she was totally unacquainted with work of any kind.

"You're frowning."

"Why did you sit here?"

Pippa's brows pleated at the sudden return of the sting in his verbal tail. "I told you. I'm researching and you're exactly what I need. I really am J. B. Starr. I'd show you some ID but unfortunately, J. B. is my pseudonym."

"Why me?" he demanded, still not believing her, not because he didn't recognize the name but because he did. He read Starr's books as well. No way was this creature the writer of the intricately woven tales that were his one and only relaxation.

"Your walk. It's fabulous."

"That is definitely a new line."

Pippa chuckled, suddenly realizing where his mind had strayed. "You think I'm trying to pick you up. Gold digger or lady of the evening?"

"I hadn't decided," he admitted abruptly. At the very least he had expected anger, not this amused acceptance.

Pippa propped her chin in her hand and rested her elbow on the seat arm. She was close enough to feel the heat of his body and respond to the scent of his cologne. Both called to the woman rather than the writer.

"Don't you think you ought to have?" she asked, studying him, wishing they were going on the same cruise. Getting to know him sounded like the most exciting thing she had contemplated in years. His control was staggering, and a challenge she could hardly resist even now.

"The trip barely makes the question a problem."

Josh stared into her eyes and wished he hadn't. There were secrets hiding in the sky-colored depths, fantasies to match his own experience and passion. Wanting, unashamedly vivid and erotically honest, warmed his blood. He cleared his throat, forcing himself to look away.

"I bother you," Pippa said softly.

"You'd bother a sainted eunuch," he growled, disturbed at his lapse. He had meant to while away a few moments out of time, not fall into a pit of his own needs.

What Pippa would have replied was lost in the captain's announcement that they had reached their destination. The seat-belt sign came on and with it a return of sanity for Josh.

"I never did get your name," Pippa murmured, just as the plane touched down.

"Joshua Luck." Josh looked at her, surprised at the flash of pleasure in her eyes.

Now, she had an explanation for that vague sense of having seen him before. Joseph Luck's picture had been part of the package that Miriam had emailed her. There couldn't be that many people with that name, Pippa thought, remembering the head speaker on the cruise. It was uncanny how much the two men resembled each other.

The didn't just share a last name. The same dark hair and chiseled features with only the look in their eyes being the telling difference. Joshua's gaze was analytical, bold, self-assured.

Joseph's pictured look was calm but with a depth that promised this many looked at the world in ways that most never knew.

"Are you going to Tampa for business?" she asked carefully, wondering if Fate had just dropped a lovely bonus in her lap. What if Joshua Luck was going on the cruise with his brother?

"Pleasure." He watched the smile in her eyes touch her lips. "You look like someone just declared today was Christmas," he said, uneasy without being sure why.

"Maybe they have. It's my favorite holiday, after all."

Pippa glanced out the window, for once oblivious to the plane and the passengers. The next two weeks promised to hold a wealth of new experiences, and she couldn't wait to begin them.

Anticipation shivered through her for the days ahead. Fate couldn't possibly be unkind enough to drop Joshua Luck in front of her and then snatch him away.

She could just ask him if he was going to be on the cruise. She laughed mentally at the thought. Nope, she was going to let this little twist in her life play out without any help from her.

At least not yet.

CHAPTER FOUR

Pippa tipped the cabin steward, giving him a smile that guaranteed her perfect service for the duration of the voyage. Excitement was champagne in her blood. Unpacking could wait. Taking only time enough to tuck her laptop safely in a drawer, she zipped out of her cabin to watch the boarding of the rest of the passengers from the rail.

Anticipation all but sizzled in the air. Smiles, quick laughter, people hurrying in a chaotic rainbow of emotion. She loved it.

As yet she hadn't seen Joshua Luck nor the man she hoped was his brother. Mentally crossing her fingers, she leaned over the rail and scanned the faces coming on board. Suddenly her eye caught a flash of plain brown wrapped around a slender female figure in the line of gaily dressed people.

The ordinary colors stood out as a more spectacular shade would not have. Her curiosity piqued, Pippa followed the progress of the young woman as she came on board, alone, quiet, with a kind of sadness about her that touched Pippa's soft heart. She wasn't smiling as she sidestepped any accidental contact with those around her. When the girl came close, Pippa realized that she wasn't a girl at all.

Although her eyes were tired, drained of life, the pretty pale face belonged to someone in her late twenties. The body was much too thin, as though the owner was ill or recuperating. Just at that moment, the large handbag the woman carried was knocked from her grasp, spilling its contents all over the deck.

No one seemed to notice the woman, only the mess she was trying desperately to clean up. The crowd around her parted just enough to avoid the stuff on the deck. No one stopped. No one offered to help.

Pippa moved forward through the crowd, stopping close enough to use her body to protect the woman while she tried collect her things.

"Let me help you," Pippa said, smiling gently as she leaned down to retrieve a cell phone. Almost at once two men and another woman joined her in gathering the scattered belongings.

"Oh, no, I couldn't," a hesitant voice whispered as the woman thrust items into her bag with no attempt at order. Her cheeks were pink, the first touch of life in her appearance.

Pippa and her helpers made quick work of the job despite the protest. Pippa thanked the trio with a smile and a quick word, then turned to the woman now standing beside her as though she didn't know where to go.

"I'm Pippa."

The woman stared at the vision in front of her, wishing she knew where her cabin was. Being out in the open this way was frightening. Someone might recognize her. No one knew where she was but that didn't mean that the people around her didn't keep up with the news and the trial.

"Lyla," she answered, using only her first name. She looked around, trying to decide where she was and how to find her cabin.

Pippa frowned slightly. Lyla looked hunted. "Are you lost?" she asked carefully.

"I usually am." Lyla flushed, then shrugged. Because Pippa had been kind, she tried a smile. "I really am all right. I just look dense."

Pippa frowned at the unswerving certainty in the soft voice. Dense would have been the last adjective she would have applied to this fragile creature. Closeup she looked exhausted, at the end of her emotional, possibly even physical reserves.

"Well, actually, I was trying to strike up an acquaintance," Pippa confessed, lying without a qualm.

Instinct told her that Lyla was in some kind of trouble. Pippa could no more resist trying to help than she could have stopped the sun from rising in the east.

"You and I look like the only people on this ship not traveling with a companion. My travel agent didn't tell me this would be a single person's nightmare."

Lyla glanced about, seeing the truth in Pippa's observation. She had been so intent on getting on board without being recognized that she hadn't really paid any attention to her companions on the voyage.

Pippa slipped on her most deprecating smile. "Somehow I always attract the most unusual males. The last trip, some silly Arab tried to convince me that I wanted to be wife number five. I ask you, what self-respecting equal-rights female would want to wait fifth in line for some man? The least he could have done was offer me the top spot," she added indignantly.

Lyla surprised them both with a quick laugh. "Maybe his eyesight was going," she offered, responding to Pippa's warmth. It had been so long since anyone had been kind to her.

Pippa pretended to give the matter some thought. "Maybe. He had to be over sixty anyway. Women my age have to expect the old fools now and again, I suppose."

Pippa edged out into the line of traffic. "Tell me you're staying on the Navigation deck. That is unless you'd rather pretend that we haven't met? I do tend to make people nervous."

Lyla smiled shakily, charmed, touched, and, without knowing it, falling completely under Pippa's spell. "I am on the Navigation deck, and I would like to know you."

Pippa grinned. "Come on then. Luckily one of the stewards took pity on me and showed me where to go. Otherwise, I would have been wandering around like a lost dog for the duration."

She tucked her arm in Lyla's, ignoring the quick stiffening of her body. Her expression showed not a care while her agile mind sifted through the possible explanations for Lyla's nervous behavior. None were reassuring and all were teases for her curiosity.

"Let's get you settled."

Josh surveyed his cabin for a moment, before starting on the chore of unpacking. Traveling had taught him the value of having a system of clothes placement so that time spent looking for his socks and other such items was at a minimum.

His movements controlled, precise, he made short work of the task. Even as his hands were occupied so, too, was his mind. This first meeting with Joe would set the tone for the cruise. He wanted the best possible beginning for both their sakes. The past was dead and he intended it to stay buried.

Less than a half hour after arrival and without making an adjustment to his businessman's attire, he left his cabin. The purser had provided him with Joe's cabin number and a map of the layout of the ship. He utilized both without mishap. Knocking on the door, he waited for Joe to answer.

The panel opened and he stood looking at his brother. Neither spoke immediately, both aware of the past and the unwritten future. The Luck clan had bred true to the influence of their paternal side. Both Josh and Joe were of the same height, breadth, and weight. Their hair was the same dense shade of black, their eyes the same rich brown.

Despite the fifteen-year difference in their ages, when they were together, strangers had often had difficulty in telling me apart. However, for those who knew them well, the were a number of differences.

No expression ever showed in Josh's eyes while Joe's were a mirror of compassion and gentleness. His told the seeker that he would never be shocked by the less kind side of life and that infinite patience was just waiting for the need to arise. His voice was gentle too, slow, easy without the authoritative edge of Josh's. His walk was more fluid, a long-legged stride that hardly disturbed the air around him. Josh's walk was all confidence and assurance. He was a success and he knew it.

"I didn't think it would be so difficult," Josh said finally.

Joe shook his head, grimacing. "Neither did I." He stepped back, gesturing Josh inside. "I tried to prepare myself if something came up at the last minute and you couldn't come. I'm not sure whether I would have been glad or sorry."

Josh took a chair, his face matching his brother's expression. "Same here. We're both stubborn fools."

Joe gave a short crack of humorless laughter. "We had a good teacher."

Josh inclined his head. Age had given him the wisdom and the hindsight to know what their parent had done. "Yes, Father did his best to destroy us and our relationship."

"He succeeded for a while." Joe went to the bar and poured himself a drink. He had thought himself past bitterness and found now that he was not. "Do you want one?"

"If that's Scotch, yes."

Joe took him a glass. "I never realized you knew what Father was doing. You seemed to be so much like him there at the last."

"We shared the same interests. That was our only meeting point." Josh shrugged impatiently. "Besides, one of us had to take the damn business over with him incapacitated like he was. There were people depending on us for their livelihood."

"And I couldn't." Joe looked down at his drink.

"It wasn't your field and never had been. I understood that even if he didn't. I really didn't mind that part. What bothered me was that damn proxy fight when you handed over your shares to the opposition."

The words drowned his good intentions and breathed life into the memory of the blood and sweat that he had poured into the company right after his father's death. The sudden news that Joe had thrown in his lot with those who sought to keep him off the board had been a blow he had not seen coming. The hurt, the sense of betrayal was no less now than then.

"I didn't do it, Josh."

Josh's eyes were brown flint when he raised them to Joe's face. "Really? You were the only holding those votes. If not you, who?"

"Father."

The sword fell between them, the human sword that had always separated them. "How? Why?"

"How was easy. It was an automatic set-up with his lawyer. One you never had to know of. The why is equally obvious. He wanted to make sure that neither of us could ever come to the other again. He hated me and he loved you. It was and is that simple."

Josh got to his feet, struggling to see past what he had believed all these years to the brutal truth of the enigma of their parent.

"It doesn't wash, Joe. We've both known Brett Thompson for years. He would have told me. He knew how I felt about what you had done."

"When I realized what Father had willed me to do, I threatened to refuse any inheritance at all. The rider was that if I did that, every share would be sold at below market to your largest competitor. You would have had no chance at all then. I had to go through with the will as written.

The threat Father held over Thompson was a loan he had needed when his wife had taken ill. But for Father the man would have been wiped out. Father refused to ever accept a penny of the money back. In return, Brett had to guarantee his silence for five years after his death. This is the last year. He can provide the proof now."

Josh stared at Joe, finally finding answers to the riddles of the past. But in the answers were simply more questions. "Why would he want me to lose the company?"

Joe's lips twisted grimly. "That's the most diabolical part of this whole thing. It is the one thing Brett and I counted on even when it looked as though I was cutting your throat.

Father had taught you so well that you were even better in a corporate fight than he. He never expected you to lose and neither did we. You got angry, cold-bloodedly angry and took on the opposition. You wiped them out. In the process it gave you a reason to hate me. The irony of the mess was that you never did. It ruined our relationship but I never felt that you hated me."

Joe looked away, then back. "I don't think I can tell you what that meant to me."

Josh got to his feet and paced to the porthole. He could hear the lighthearted chaos of those embarking on well-deserved vacations.

"I wanted to," he admitted quietly. "I kept telling myself I should, but somehow I could never stop hoping for one lousy reason why."

He shrugged, angry at the past and the man who no one had ever really understood until it was too late.

"But you didn't. In the end, Father didn't win."

"No, but he stole years from us." Josh turned on his heel to face Joe, unprepared to be as forgiving as his brother.

"Maybe it will only make us value the future more." Joe came to him. "If you hadn't called me, I was going to come to you after the cruise, Brett and I both, with the papers if necessary to prove what happened back then." He held out his hand. "Thank you for not needing them."

Josh looked at the gesture, grinned crookedly, feeling young again. He took the hand and used it to pull Joe close. Neither man was given to displays of affection, but this once, it was important to touch as the innocent children they had once been.

"Welcome back brother."

Joe laughed, tipping his head as he stepped out of the man hug they had shared. "It feels good. I'm ready to celebrate." For an instant his mood dimmed. "I dreaded this, you know."

Josh found he could laugh now himself. "The famed psychic didn't know how it was going to go down?"

"I never have been able to see all that well for myself."

"Do you think you can see for me?"

Both men were startled at the impulsive words. "I have no idea," Joe replied curiously. "Why the sudden interest in the future?"

Josh shrugged uncomfortably. "Forget I said anything. The timing is off anyway."

Joe frowned, studying his brother, seeing a faint uncertainty where there had only been clear-sighted purpose in the past.

"What is it, Josh? Don't shut me out. We've spent years doing that to each other. Let me help."

"I'm not sure you can."

Joe waited, sensing more would come. "Do you ever wish you weren't alone?"

"Constantly. You haven't married either?" The last was a statement that was really a question. The words were subtle, respecting Joe's right to privacy.

"I was close once, but the woman couldn't take my oddness." He smiled, unaware of the bitterness in his gesture. "Her words, not mine. It wasn't her reaction that bothered me, because that is usually the reaction after the newness of being with a psychic loses its shine. It was the fact she knew I was serious and she knew that I thought she was, too. She wasn't and never had been. "

"Damn, Joe, I'm sorry. "

"Don't be. Other than her timing, which was right during that proxy thing, she did me a favor. I know better now." He moved to the bar and poured himself another short drink. "The thought occurs that for two estranged brothers and ones not given to many confidences in the best of circumstances, we're doing a great deal of confiding."

"If your situation is anything like mine, who else would you tell?"

Joe glanced at him, inclining his head. "Good point, big brother. Who else indeed?" He lifted his glass. "So, tell me what brought this curiosity about my love life and your own to the floor. I thought you and Lisa were a thing. The papers certainly think so."

Josh gave a short, humorless laugh. "That is the one thing we're not. A thing. We're relaxing and pleasant. Apparently at my age that's all I can hope for, according to the lady. "

Joe surprised him with a graphic comment on Lisa's powers of observation. "I hope you got rid of her."

"I wouldn't put it quite that way, but let's say I did extradite myself from the situation."

"So now what?"

"I believe that's what I asked you."

"You were serious? You really want a reading?"

"Don't make it sound so damn farfetched. You do it for other people. "

Joe wasn't sure why he was hesitating. "Josh, I never gloss over what I see. You may be opening more of a can of worms than our current relationship can tolerate."

Josh hadn't considered that aspect. He had forgotten his brother's bone-deep honesty and truth, at-all-costs belief. Maybe he didn't want to know the future. Maybe that was just more of his staid and cautious personality coming through.

"Maybe you're right." he said slowly. "Maybe, for once in my life, I should obey my impulses. At least for two weeks."

"You with an impulse?"

Josh's brows raised at the skeptical note. "You don't think I can have one?"

"Neither of us is given to jumping first then asking questions. I'd have more luck and am more flexible than you."

What was it with the people who thought they knew him? Was he that damn predictable? The more he saw himself through others' eyes the less he liked.

"You are beginning to remind me strongly of Lisa," he warned irritably.

"A fate worse than death." Amused, Joe clapped him on the back. "Why don't you just try for a little relaxation?"

"I like impulsive better," Josh said stubbornly, heading for the door. "In fact, the more I think about it the better I like it all together."

Joe followed, chuckling. "I suppose this impulse will have to include a woman."

"It might. I don't know yet."

"I think this cruise is going to prove to be most enlightening for both of us. I think I would just as soon not see the future."

Pippa and Lyla wandered along the deck, periodically stopping to enjoy the scenery. People having fun, laughing and getting to know one another were everywhere. Bright colors, music, happy voices.

Occasionally, when she was sure Lyla wasn't looking, Pippa studied the younger woman. She didn't talk much. Her movements were graceful but so filled with tension that she looked almost awkward.

Despite her growing need to solve the riddle of Lyla, Pippa knew the value of patience. The last thing she wanted to do was drive Lyla back into her shell. It had taken a great deal of persuasion to convince Lyla to leave her cabin to watch the ship leave the dock.

So she waited, occupying her mind with thoughts of Joshua Luck. She had come on board, half bored with her life and needing a challenge.

She had found two problems, unrelated but equally demanding in their own way. One would be a lot of work, but the other, Joshua Luck, if he was on board, would be pure enjoyment.

"How many Lucks can there be?" she muttered under her breath. The resemblance had been too marked to be a fluke.

"I beg your pardon?"

Pippa smiled ruefully at the young waiter who stopped before them. "Talking to myself."

He grinned, his blue eyes sparkling with masculine appreciation. He hardly glanced at Lyla." "You can't be alone."

"Unfortunately, I am."

"It's got to be out of choice."

Pippa laughed softly, aware that Lyla was slowly edging out of the way. It was clear she intended to fade into the deck if possible.

"Watch it. I'm much too old for you."

The game was fun. This young man knew the rules and the moves. His expression said he really did like what he saw but that he wasn't going to take advantage of the fact or her.

He didn't look upset at the prospect. "Age is in the mind."

"Really?" Her brows arched, waiting for the next volley, even as she watched Lyla's reaction.

Just at that moment, Joshua and Joe rounded the comer of the deck. Both men stopped, Josh because the last thing he wanted was to be discovered by that female hunter in the sexy packaging.

Joseph, because the laughter of the woman before him had such a joy in it that he couldn't resist stopping to share the moment of an innocent flirtation. Neither man noticed Lyla as she stood in the shadow of the stairway to the next deck.

"Of all the rotten luck," Josh mumbled.

Joe cast him a startled look. "What are you talking about?"

"That woman. She's the one I told you about who tried to pick me up on the plane. Look at her. She could give that kid twenty years and change."

"That kid is Tony and he's twenty-eight years old. That would put your lady at your exalted age, older brother."

He chuckled at the dirty look he received. "She doesn't look like a man-hunter to me. Just seems like she's having some harmless fun, and I happen to know Tony isn't into playing around with the lady passengers. He likes his job too much and he has a pretty little waitress in the main dining room he's trying to get to take him seriously."

"Don't tell me all that came out of your crystal ball."

"No, that came straight from the horse's mouth during the last cruise." Joe started forward. "Come on. We can't stand here blocking the deck forever. I'm here. I'll protect you from the lady."

Josh followed. "Cute, younger brother, cute. You weren't the one she singled out so damn obviously that the whole plane knew what was coming down."

"Hiya, Joe," Tony said, catching sight of his friend.

Pippa turned, her eyes lighting at the appearance of Joshua Luck with a man beside him who could be his clone. Joseph Luck, no doubt. "You are on this cruise."

"Obviously," Josh replied, trying to deflect her. That intense look in her eyes was becoming all too familiar. But more familiar still was his body's recognition of her appeal. Her scent was on the breeze, teasing him, promising things he would be a fool to accept.

"I'm Joseph Luck," Joe said holding out his hand.

Blinking at the interruption, Pippa turned slightly. She gave him her hand, studying his face, finding in it the same genetic looks and eye color but not the same impact.

Josh had a commanding presence that was evident in every separate feature. Joe was the opposite end of the spectrum. His eyes held gentleness, infinite understanding, and a kind of wry humor that appealed to her. Her gaze slipped past him to Lyla, who looked as though she desperately needed to run.

Pippa noted the reaction and stifled the urge to bring Lyla to the attention of the men. "Alike but very different. Are you close?" she murmured, angling her body so that Lyla was even less in the line of vision. The urge to protect was as natural as breathing.

Josh watched them, seeing the way that neither made any attempt to let go of their hands. "Do you have some contractual agreement with the world to ask nosy questions of complete strangers?" he demanded.

"I ask because I want to know. No one is forced to answer," she said without turning her head.

"She's got you there, Josh."

"Don't help her or you'll find yourself with a new assistant."

"You say that with all the horror of someone discussing the black plague." She turned to Josh then, her eyes alight with a wicked desire to tease. "Admit it. I made the hop from Jacksonville to Tampa seem a lot shorter than it was."

Before Josh could respond, Tony spoke. "Now that you've got these two, I'd better get to work."

Tony cast an expert eye over the passengers beginning to settle on deck near the pool. "Have a good trip." He gave Pippa a hundred-watt smile which she returned.

Josh frowned irritably, wondering why it bothered him what this crazy, uninhibited woman was up to and with whom.

"Don't we have some place to be Joe?" he murmured, hinting broadly.

Joe looked so startled that Pippa laughed. "You should always clue a partner in on the small signs of polite fiction," she observed.

Josh bit back an oath. Playing this woman's game hadn't gotten him anywhere so far. "We wouldn't want to take up your time. You must have things to do."

"Does he ever unbend just a little?" she asked Joe.

Joe kept a straight face with effort. He could tell that Pippa knew she was getting to Josh. She understood his barbs, was amused by them, and clearly determined to face more if necessary. What he couldn't figure out was why.

The one thing he did know was that Josh had the wrong end of the stick thinking this creature was a lady of the night or a woman on the make. She might know all the moves but the sexuality for monetary gain simply wasn't there. Her game was something else altogether different.

"When he was younger," he answered slowly, studying Pippa and trying to understand her. His powers, instincts, or whatever the thinking world called them, told him to strengthen the connection between himself, Josh, and this woman.

Left to Josh, he knew the tie would be broken. His brother was not given to being chased, regardless of the reasons.

"If you two are going to talk about me as if I were not here, I'm leaving you to it. I do have other things to do." Without waiting for a rebuttal, Josh left them. Joe watched him go, frowning. "I better not have made a mistake."

Pippa didn't need the t's crossed to know what he meant. "He thinks I'm trying to angle my way into his bed."

Joe studied her shrewdly. "Why aren't you? He's wealthy, attractive, and single."

"And he isn't into relationships any more than I am."

"That must have been one informative plane ride."

So he had confided in his brother about their time together on the plane. Interesting. She wouldn't have thought him the type to kiss and tell.

"You know better. Your brother could give a clam lessons. I just happen to make my living reading people."

Joe looked closer. It hadn't occurred to him that she was psychic. "I didn't realize. You must be new to our field."

Pippa's brow creased in puzzlement for a moment, then she chuckled delightedly. "No, I don't mean I read futures or anything like that. I'm a writer. I read characters, people, humanity, that kind of thing. Your brother couldn't be more obvious if he wore a sign. Besides, like I said, as cliche as it sounds, it takes one to know one. "

"Then what do you want from him?"

Pippa linked her arm with his. One discreet glance to Lyla's tense face told her what she should do. It was time to take Joe away before he noticed the woman edging toward the door behind her.

She really wanted to introduce Lyla, bring her into the conversation but Lyla was looking strained again, edgy, almost afraid. Until she knew understood what or who was hunting Lyla, she would do all that she could to protect her.

She eased away from Lyla, giving her enough room to escape if that was what she really wanted. She was aware the moment that Lyla slipped through the doorway to one of the small eateries.

"I'll make a deal with you. I'll tell you what I want with your brother if you'll tell me about being a psychic. I've been writing about it for years, reading books on the subject, and I've even talked with a few self-styled fortune tellers, but you're the first real thing I've ever met.

In short, my writer's curiosity is aroused, and when it's in ascension, it needs to be satisfied for me to be happy."

Joe looked into her eyes, expecting to see the laughter he was coming to associate with her. Instead, he saw her clear-sighted purpose, steel beneath the velvet-and-pearl body, and a kind of honesty rare to the human race. It was then that he knew he liked her and that he could trust her.

"Deal. Which of us goes first?"

"You?" she said promptly.

"I wonder why I expected that answer."

"Psychic?"

"No. This time I didn't need it. For a complex lady you can be amazingly straightforward."

"Not a bad assessment for such a short acquaintance."

He dipped his head, his eyes gleaming with laughter. For the first time in a long while, he was truly enjoying himself. "I can see why Josh is running a mile to avoid you. You're addictive, Pippa."

"I'm also impossible," she added, smiling. "I have it on the best authority."

"Male, no doubt."

"Jason. My nephew. As I recall, he was shouting, and Jason never shouts, about sticking my nose into his wedding. I had to remind him but for me there wouldn't be a wedding."

Joe shook his head, fascinated by her words and the expressions chasing across her face. "What happened?"

"I won, of course. I always do."

"So does Joshua," he warned.

She stopped, looking him in the eye, her own steady, unreadable for once. "But you see, I'm not playing a game with your brother."

CHAPTER FIVE

Joshua walked the circuit of the promenade deck, blind to the sea, the white cotton clouds overhead, and the other passengers. For a man who had led a surprisingly smooth personal life, he had, in a few short hours, run head first into an obstacle that was unlike anything he had ever encountered.

Pippa, what a name, was not the kind of woman he should be attracted to, but he was. She was bizarre, to say the least. He wasn't certain he even knew what she was. Hell, he wasn't even certain she knew what she was.

And Joe, he had looked altogether too taken with his sexy nemesis. The last thing they needed at this juncture of their relationship was a problem with a woman. So what now? he asked himself silently.

Pippa didn't look the type of woman to be discouraged by anything less than a blunt weapon. He stopped at the rail, staring out across the water. He was still standing there when Pippa found him.

She stood in the shadow of the overhang, watching Josh, admiring the clean lines of his elegant body. His stillness was almost as eye riveting as his walk. Her lips curved secretively as she moved toward him. She knew the moment he sensed her presence.

"You don't need to tense up. I came to make peace," she murmured, pausing beside him. She was close enough to touch, but she didn't shorten the distance with human contact.

Josh glanced at her, intending only to send her away. Something in her expression stopped him. This was not the woman he had met on the plane or the one he had walked away from laughing, with Joe on her arm.

"What kind of peace?" he asked warily.

Pippa ignored the question she wasn't ready to answer. "You think I'm after your money or you. I'm not. Not in the way you mean, anyway, so you can relax. I told you the truth on the plane. You would make a marvelous prototype for my next hero. All I want is to follow you around for a few hours, ask a few questions so that I can understand how you think, and then I'll disappear out of your life."

She hesitated, wondering if anything she was saying was reaching behind that unreadable face. "I'll probably end up chin-deep in a new story before this voyage is over, and I promise you, I could even provide unimpeachable witnesses if we were home, that I am the next best thing to a recluse when I'm on the trail of a plot."

Joshua studied the determined glint in her eyes, suspecting that if he refused this olive branch, she would just find another way to get her material. Assuming she was telling him the truth. This woman didn't appear to understand or acknowledge the word no.

"I came on this trip for a vacation."

"I won't interfere with that," she said quickly, sensing a capitulation in the offing.

He just looked at her, wondering if she was being deliberately dense.

Pippa grinned, realizing that the man was actually trying to find a way to tell her that he wasn't adverse to a little female companionship and didn't want a chaperone. "I promise I won't look."

He frowned and she laughed. With the sound came a slam of desire to his midsection and lower. Josh accepted the blow, his face as smooth as the gleaming metal of the rail beneath his hands.

Her scent was all around, beckoning, promising, tantalizing him to forget his caution and go for the woman. This was impulse in capital letters, a gift of a maniacal god.

"Did anyone ever threaten you with bodily injury?"

Somehow, he had to make her want to walk away. Even as the thought occurred, he moved a step closer, his nostrils flaring, drinking in the fragrance of the hunter, the spinner of the web of need that was slowly trapping him on a path he hadn't chosen.

"Frequently, but so far I have emerged unscathed from all retribution. You remind me of Jason."

He had to break the tie. "Your lover?"

"My nephew."

The first cut was done, now for the last. "Good word for it." He waited for her anger and got another of those sexy chuckles that gave him ideas better suited for the bedroom. The woman was impervious to insult.

"Jason would die laughing at the thought, and then he would kill me for just thinking about it. I drive him nuts. In fact, I usually do drive every male in my circle nuts."

She shrugged, totally undisturbed at the prospect. "I don't fit the mold you see. I do what I want, when I want, with whom I want. A gypsy, a vagabond, a wanderer. Round peg in a square hole."

Pippa was so accustomed to living in her odd-at-all-costs world that she didn't hear the underlying sadness, the bewildered hurt of never truly belonging that colored her voice.

But Joshua, the man who rarely saw beyond the facts and figures of a given situation, did hear. He closed his lips on the final thrust of the conversation and looked deep into another human being for the first time in his experienced life. Then he surprised them both by taking her hand in his, holding it as one would something infinitely fragile.

"There is nothing round or square about you. Curved delightfully, intricately molded by a creator of rare beauty." For one who had no poetry in his soul, his words were verbal beauty to soothe the past into a dim memory.

Pippa froze, the sun suddenly cold compared to the heat in Josh's brown eyes. "Compliments," she tried to joke, feeling vulnerable when she never had before. Men were wondrous creatures...strong, intriguing, complex, but seldom kind.

With his free hand he touched her cheek, drawing a finger along the elegant curve. Desire was the spice in his thoughts but not a demand. This woman was unique, a person as well as a mind and a body. He wanted to know more. Her forthright approach appealed to his own logic. Her smile drew him closer, but it was her multifaceted personality that kept him in front of her.

"Truth. You look in the mirror, you live in this body, you use this mind. You aren't subtle."

She smiled, knowing that she was very subtle indeed, although, just this once, she hadn't used that talent. She was reacting, rather than initiating. She was allowing a man to lead her. Interesting, she would have murmured, had she been in an introspective mood. For now, it was enough that he touched her.

"You might be wrong."

"I rarely am."

There it was. That wonderful regality of decision, that perfect assurance that was a step above and beyond common arrogance. She smiled, beguiled, intrigued, and imprisoned by her own curiosity. This trip was more than she could have hoped.

"Perhaps. But then again, perhaps not." She pulled her hand from his, surprised at the strength it took for the simple gesture. "We shall see," she added as she turned and walked away.

Joshua let her go because her action took him unaware. Frowning at the puzzle of the woman, he wandered down the deck, watching as Pippa walked before him. When she stopped to speak to those who spoke to her, he halted as well.

Her face was a study in moods, no two the same. Her voice was in turns seductive, amused, serious, and without expression. For the life of him he couldn't decide which was the real Pippa. When they entered the interior of the ship and the corridor around them was empty, he caught up with her.

Pippa glanced at him out of the corner of her eyes. "Is this your deck?"

Joshua looked around, then nodded. "Yes."

"But you weren't sure."

"No."

"Why?"

"Do you want me to admit that I was following you?"

"Were you?" She stopped, turning to face him. Her cabin door was at her back.

"Yes."

Pippa tipped her head, studying him, the situation, and herself. Where he had jumped to conclusions on the plane, she would not here.

"Why?"

He laughed, the sound half exasperation and the rest amusement. "And I thought you were a woman who knew the rules."

"There are rules and then there are rules." She waited.

He leaned his shoulder against the wall. He was close enough to touch her, but he resisted the temptation. "How did you get the cabin across from mine? Accident or design?"

"Which do you think?"

He studied her face, finding no clue in her eyes. Intuition beyond a business scope was as new as the rest of his emotions, just as uncomfortable.

"Accident," he said finally.

Pippa stroked his cheek, patting it, laughing into his startled eyes. Touching her forefinger to her lips, she licked it and then drew an imaginary one in the air.

"You're improving."

He caught her hand, tumbling her against his chest. He had never been one to take a dare just because it was there. He looked and studied before he acted. Until this woman.

"Damn you. Why couldn't you have found someone else to plague?" he groaned, taking her mouth.

Pippa didn't fight the primitive gesture or the man who made it. She wanted to know his taste as much as it seemed he wanted hers. He was hard, his body tight and warm against hers.

His mouth was a demand, calling to the passion uncurling like an awakened cat within her. The claws flashed out of velvet sheaths, sinking into the fabric of her mind, bringing desire alive. Her hands slipped to his shoulders, binding him to her as her tongue dueled with his. His scent was heady, teasing her closer.

Joshua felt the impact of Pippa's kiss all the way to his shoes. He had never known such unrestrained emotion that was more than sexual need in his life. Her body was living fire in his hands, her fragrance a mixture of subtle woman and blatant hunter.

He had no defense, for he had not known the danger. Even as his logical mind shouted beware, his fingers molded her to him, taking the wine of passion from her lips, tasting it, inhaling its bouquet, and growing drunk with its punch. Her groan, soft, husky with need, tore at his control.

"Your keys," he commanded, edging her closer to her door.

Pippa blinked, her eyes focusing on the blazing features so close to her own. "What?"

"Your keys. Privacy." Josh bent his head to trace a line of kisses down her throat. Her skin was satin and velvet. He had to have more.

Pippa held his head to her for one instant, staring down the empty corridor without really seeing it. Fighting herself was a new experience, but her mind had always been her strength. Slamming the lid on her passion, she lifted his head in her hands. If it was a close call on winning the battle, no one but she would know.

"No," she said distinctly.

Josh stared at her, for one second suspecting a game of tease and deny. The smoldering look in her eyes told a different story.

"Why?"

"We don't know each other."

"I want you."

"Not enough."

His brows raised at the indifference that wasn't feigned in her voice. "Any more and I would have burned this ship down. And you're a liar if you say you weren't in a similar predicament."

"Passion is easy."

"Maybe for you," Josh replied smartly before he thought.

She smiled faintly. She ignored the sting of his quick rebuttal. "For you, too. Whoever told you differently was lying. Or was it your partner talking about herself?"

Josh shrugged, taking a single step back from the heat and the demand of her body. Uncomfortable with her insight, angered at his own vulnerability, he tossed a verbal block between them.

"It doesn't matter."

She touched his arm. Though he was trying to close her out she had had too much experience with Jason's attempts to lock her out of his thoughts to lose with this man.

"It does, but now is not the time for us to go into that."

He looked at her, for the first time since he had met her, reverting to type. His expression smoothed, his emotions icing over. Her words were so like those of his youth when a man, his father, had treated him as nothing more than an unthinking robot. He had been too young to defend himself then. He was no longer.

"I thought you were a writer. Not an analyst."

Pippa felt the bite of his anger, although nothing showed on his face. Hurt was rolling off him in waves. She could have drowned in it or ridden the tide to the island of feminine sympathy. She chose neither course. She looked him in the eye, challenging him.

"Sting me and I'll sting back. You kissed me, not the other way around. Yes, I want you, but contrary to your rather interesting opinion of me, I don't jump into bed with the first man to stir my hormones.

Sexy as you are, I need more. Sex for its own sake is bread without a damn thing to go with it. It's interesting in the first flash of intensity, then boring and easily forgotten."

Pippa reached in her pocket and pulled out her keys. "You want a quick tumble? Find a susceptible female and give her one of those passionate looks. She'll probably flop at your feet like a landed fish," she added, jamming the key in the lock and turning it with a jerk.

Josh caught her arm before she could slam the door in his face. "Why are you angry?"

Pippa stared into his eyes, wondering the same thing herself. Losing her temper was a rare occurrence. But then the day had been filled with oddities.

"I have no idea. But believe me I won't lose any sleep over the situation." She pulled her arm out of his grip, shot him a dark look, and closed the door with enough force to be heard.

Josh glared at the blank panel, not sure what had happened but definitely certain that this wasn't the end of the encounter. He had come on this trip to reassess his life, to reconnect with his brother.

He had not come on this voyage to give in to an impulse, enjoy a woman who didn't add life on an invisible tally sheet. The last thought stopped him in his mental tracks. Where had that come from? He frowned, realizing that his relationship with Lisa had just that kind of flavor. Nothing at all like Pippa. Lisa was safe. No demands for time or emotion to disturb the main focus of his life. His work.

Pippa was a challenge, an enigma, an enchantress, and a hunter. The guises were as multifaceted as her moods. Also, as impossible to predict. He had these two short weeks. Why not enjoy them for what they were. A vacation, a time for indulging himself in ways he never had before. His real life was onshore. He accepted that this time would end.

Suddenly, a smile touched his lips, his eyes taking on the gleam of the devil himself. Pulling his keys from his pocket, he crossed the corridor and opened his door. A few moments later he had arranged his little surprise. Pippa had caught him flat-footed. Now it was his turn.

CHAPTER SIX

Pippa stared at her reflection, stunned at the change a few moments of passion could make. "Damn," she swore angrily.

Emotion bottled was a potent force. Pippa fought herself, staring at the fine trembling in her hands with something akin to fury. "I will not be caught in this trap. Passion is fun, laughter, sometimes shared interests. Not hunger!"

But it was hunger. Even as she denied it, she knew the truth. She had watched Jason, Diana, Lorelei, and Alex. Such need had been within each, such pain, such longing that couldn't be denied. Marriage had been their answer.

But for her, such a step was a trap. A place of confinement. A demand for dependability. Someone else needs placed before her own. Changes to the life she had constructed for herself.

"I can't do it," she whispered to the empty room.

Who is asking you to? a voice inside her head responded bluntly. Pippa froze, her eyes dilating with shock. Why had she thought marriage? A natural progression for many? Not for her.

Nothing about Joshua indicated he was any more enamored of that lovely institution than she. Slowly, she relaxed, sanity driving a balancing wedge into her seesaw reactions. Breathing deeply, she willed her body to quiet. Desire reluctantly curled within itself.

Pippa would have liked to have known it was gone but she accepted it simply slept until the next time. But it would be different then. She would be ready.

She would understand that her need was greater than those she had experienced in the past. She could accept that, deal with it, perhaps even allow it to hold sway for a few precious days. But then it would die, as it always did, and her life would return to normal.

"Josh, it's Joe. About dinner together tonight. I'm going to be held up if I make it at all. I've got a private reading due in the next five minutes. No telling how long it will take. Go ahead without me. I'll try to make it down later. If I don't, we can meet in the Pirate Lounge and have a drink."

Josh dried his face with the hand towel as he listened to his brother's snappy explanation. He sounded almost nervous over a simple change of plans.

"No big deal. This is a working cruise for you. I don't mind working around your schedule."

Joe sighed, relaxing at Josh's easy acceptance. "I'll get better," he admitted.

Josh chuckled. "We both will. As a matter of fact, I think you might be doing me a favor. I rearranged the seating for dinner. Pippa doesn't know it yet but she's dining with us or, I should say, me now."

Joe sat down, trying not to laugh. The satisfaction in Josh's voice was unmistakable.

"I can't believe it. You mean to tell me you highhandedly set this up? Mr. Cautious and Predictable? You would do something like this when I won't be around to watch the results?"

"Into every life a little rain must fall," Josh returned lazily, dropping the towel that just barely reached around his narrow waist.

The light in the cabin gilded his tanned body to gold. With every movement the muscles rippled beneath his flesh in a dance of unbelievable grace. He reached for his shirt, shrugging into it as he talked.

"You like her, don't you?"

"I can think of a number of things I feel about that woman, but liking doesn't begin to cover the description," Josh answered honestly.

Joe's brows came together in a small frown. Some people were easily read. Pippa was not one of them. He had sensed complexities in her that didn't fit the lazy sexuality that she projected.

"Be careful, brother. She isn't what she seems."

"You mean because she's J. B. Starr. I know. She told me and I told you, remember."

"That's not what I mean," Joe said slowly, wishing he had kept his mouth shut.

For a moment, he had dropped his guard. Josh was clearly willing to try to accept him and his psychic side. That didn't mean he was ready now or even in the future to have it intrude into his life nor had he requested it.

"Forget I said anything."

Josh frowned as he sat on the edge of the bed. "Meaning?"

Joe shrugged. "I don't know, exactly. For one thing I never pry unless I'm asked. I won't break that even for you. But be careful. Pippa is a paradox, a very complex paradox. She's nothing like Lisa or the few before her."

"You don't know Lisa."

"Actually, I do. We met at a party one night, about a year before she started dating you."

Josh stared at the far wall, realizing again how distant he and Joe had been all these years.

"Thanks for meeting me halfway," he said suddenly.

Joe laughed, relief embedded in the sound. "It works both ways, big brother."

A knock at his door interrupted anything else he might have said. "My appointment's here. Got to go. Can't wait to see what comes next."

Josh hung up the phone, torn between laughing and wanting to wring his brother's neck for his amusement. "Complex paradox," he muttered.

It was as good a definition as any, he decided as he finished dressing. It would be interesting to see what Pippa did when she found out what he had done.

"What do you mean, you're not going to dinner?" Pippa asked, studying Lyla's set face.

She had knocked on Lyla's cabin door at the appointed time, expecting to find the younger woman ready to share the evening meal with her. Instead, she found Lyla in a robe, her face bare of make-up.

Lyla fiddled with the room service menu on the counter, looking anywhere but into Pippa's wise eyes. "I'm not good with strangers," she admitted, then risked a quick glance.

"Why?" Pippa replied baldly as she moved to the one of the chairs in the sitting area of the suite. With all the activity of getting onboard and settled into her cabin as well as the encounters with Joshua, she'd had little time to consider her new friend's situation.

"It's more than shyness, isn't it?" she said, watching Lyla closely. She was entirely too tense for a simple dinner invitation.

Lyla sighed deeply, knowing that for the first time in a long while she was going to confide in someone. She wasn't sure why. She wasn't sure it was a good idea but there was something about Pippa that invited confidences. Maybe she was making a mistake. She risked another quick look at Pippa's face.

She remembered how the older woman had helped her escape when they had run into the two men on deck. She had tucked her out of the way so that she didn't have meet the strangers. Pippa had even made it possible for her to leave without being obvious about it.

She had already thanked her when she had let Pippa into to the cabin. Pippa had treated the situation as though it was nothing unusual. In a way, she owed Pippa an explanation.

What did she have to lose? She was so tired of being alone. What was one more person who didn't believe her in the crowd that already existed?

"It's a complicated story."

Pippa leaned back in her chair. "I like stories and I have all the time you need."

Lyla looked at her for a moment, almost losing her nerve. But the very relaxed position and the calm expression on Pippa's face decided her. She sighed again, softer this time, and paced the room, trying to order her thoughts.

She didn't know what made her trust Pippa. The past had certainly taught her the danger of trusting anyone. But Pippa was different. There was something about her that she could depend on. It wasn't that Pippa was soft, rather just the opposite.

There was a kind of strength about her that said no matter what the world threw at her she would survive. Lyla needed that kind of belief. The past was a pile of ashes smothering her alive. She had to find a way back to the land of freedom and tomorrows.

"I'm an accountant. Or I was. Four years ago, I got this really great offer to work for an international company dealing in imports. It was like a dream come true. A company car, travel, big salary, my own office, and a chance to make a name for myself in my field. I worked hard, took on a lot of responsibility." For a moment she relived the high of finding her niche in the world.

Pippa watched the expressions slipping cross her face, reading the pride of accomplishment that hinted at the beauty that had been hers in the past. But as quick as the glimpse was there it was gone, chased away by a disillusionment that was painful to see.

"What happened?"

Lyla turned fully to face her, fear and a greater need to talk, driving the words from her.

"I was arrested for smuggling drugs. All those trips I had been making overseas had been a cover. The money I was tallying had come from the illegal parts of the operation."

Lyla paused, her face etched with confusion, a loss of innocence, and hurt. "No one believed me when I said I didn't know anything about what was going on. Everyone, my family, the media, the police, all thought that I'd had a hand in the filth because of the immediacy of my rise from a junior accountant to an important position with that kind of salary."

She lifted her chin, her eyes glazed with tears. "I don't know why I thought you would believe me."

Pippa rose and took the younger woman in her arms. Lyla held herself stiff for a moment, unable to believe Pippa's response. No one had offered her the smallest gesture of support since her world had begun crashing around her. A sob broke through her control and suddenly, she couldn't hold her pain in any longer.

Saying nothing, Pippa held Lyla as she cried against her shoulder. And, when the storm was over, she guided Lyla to a chair, moved a box of tissues closer to her hand and then went to the mini bar to pour her a drink.

"All of it," she directed when she pressed the glass into Lyla's fingers.

Lyla took it, grimacing. "I never cry," she whispered roughly. "I must seem like a baby."

Pippa dropped onto the chair across from her. She set aside the open bottle and a second, empty glass on the table between them.

"I'd say it was either cry or swear like a sailor in a case like this. I don't think swearing is your style."

Lyla managed a jerky shake of her head.

"So how did this farce end up? You're obviously free. Or have you pulled a jail break?"

Lyla stared at her in shock then choked on a laugh she didn't know she had in her. "I wouldn't have known how to escape."

Pippa frowned darkly. "Well, if you're going to be tumbling into any more messes, you'd better let me teach you the intricacies of lock-picking."

Lyla forgot her past long enough to stare at Pippa in surprise. "You know how?"

Grinning, Pippa nodded while silently congratulating herself on the random choice of conversation. Lyla was definitely losing that crushed-flower look.

"I've spent a little time in jail once. Some Italian fool decided I looked like an American tart. I could have told him I had better dress sense, but at the time I didn't speak the language all that well. Plus, I thought the macho fool was trying to make a pass at me, and when he wouldn't leave me alone, I decked him." The memory added a dash of delight to her expression.

Lyla giggled and finished the rest of her drink. For the first time in four years, she felt clean, normal, and nice. Pippa lifted the small bottle she had brought to the sitting area with her and refilled Lyla's glass.

"I don't have a head for liquor," Lyla warned, watching her.

"I never thought you did. But I want to know the rest of your little nasties, and that will be easier for you if you aren't quite sober."

"Why?"

Pippa splashed a little of the bourbon in her own glass. "So that we can set about getting you back on your feet. Watching you slink around like a criminal offends my artistic temperament, or something like that."

Lyla sipped her drink, feeling warmth slide into the cold places that the past had frozen in her soul. "Are you a good fairy?" she asked whimsically.

Pippa tipped her head back, laughing richly. "Not likely. My family will tell you I am bone-selfish and a nasty enemy. And you're right about your alcohol capacity. It's the size of a pea."

Lyla settled into the cushions, smiling. "I've never been drunk before. "

Pippa eyed the bottle and her newest project. "You aren't going to get any more. I don't want you sick for our first day in port. We are going shopping."

Lyla blinked, her body, despite the numbing effects of her tiny indulgence, tensing at the thought of being around people who might remember the scandal or recognize her. "No, I can't."

"You will. You'll even want to. I promise. Besides, no one is going to say one damn thing to you. You will have fun."

"Fun?" Lyla tasted the word, wishing it was even possible. "I can't stand the whispers. You won't be able to stop them."

Pippa's eyes narrowed, her whole face changing. A grizzly bear with a single cub would have worn such a look of intense ferocity.

"Maybe not, but I might make the comments more expensive than anyone would wish to pay. "

Lyla studied Pippa gravely. "Why me?"

Pippa didn't pretend to misunderstand. "I like challenges."

"Lost causes, more like."

"I would have said a survivor."

"I didn't have any choice."

"Didn't you? Seems to me you had quite a few. Change your name. Retreat to an addiction of some kind or any number of variations. Why did you come on this cruise?"

"It was the only thing going out of Tampa today. I came straight out of the courtroom and the guilty verdict for the man who set me up. I got a taxi to the first travel agent I found when I did a quick internet search on my cell. He had this cancellation. I took it."

She waved her hand vaguely in the direction of the small case she had brought on board with her. "I paid the cab driver to wait while I bought a few things and that over-nighter. He brought me here."

Pippa chuckled. The woman not only knew how to make decisions, but she also carried them out. "And you don't call yourself a survivor? I'd say that was smart thinking. In one stroke, you got out of the line of journalistic fire. That kind of quick cancellation means that there is a good chance that anyone looking for you is going to have a few roadblocks and it will give you time to relax and regroup."

"Impulse. There was no real thought involved."

"It works, so what difference does the name make?"

Lyla blinked owlishly as she finished the second drink. "Good point," she murmured.

"So, the bad guy got it in the end. Justice was served."

"Sort of. My reputation is shot and there isn't much chance that I'll get any kind of employment in my field now. Not with my notoriety. Even if the police finally came to the conclusion that I was a trusting fool in this mess, the rest of the world won't have all the facts."

"Now you have a blank page for a future."

Lyla opened her lips to reply before the words sank in. When they did, she hesitated. "I hadn't thought of it that way," she admitted.

"Then do. You've had a raw deal, but no amount of 'what if' is going to change that. The future is waiting for you, and it is anything and everything you can make of it. What do you want?"

"To be like you," Lyla returned promptly. surprising them both. "I want men to look at me instead of through me and I want to be different, unique. I want to travel and learn all kinds of things.

I've spent my whole life in one city, working toward one narrow goal. I followed the rules, dotted the i's, and got fried with a bunch of lies. I was so gullible that a slick businessman could use me as a pawn in a rotten drug scene. I started out clean and now I feel like I fell into a mud river. I want to breathe freely again."

She caught Pippa's hand, her voice suddenly passionate, her eyes bright, alive with a desire for life. "Can you teach me those things, Pippa? You talk of futures that I can't even see anymore. Can you help me see beyond now?"

Pippa took the thin, elegant fingers in hers. "I'll do what I can." She met Lyla's eyes, her lips wearing a slight smile. "And we'll start tomorrow."

Lyla studied her face, seeing the truth written there. Suddenly she felt as though tomorrow was possible, that the darkness of yesterday would have to give way to the sun of the future.

For the first time in years, she had hope. Tension flowed from her as water from a tipped pitcher. Her muscles relaxed. For the first time in too many nights to remember, she felt as though she could sleep without a nightmare ambush.

"I think you need sleep more than food," Pippa murmured as she stood and eased Lyla to her feet.

Swaying a little, Lyla nodded. "Breakfast in the morning?"

Pippa hugged her once more. "You bet. If you wake in the middle of the night, don't start thinking of the past. Call me and we'll wake up a steward and order snacks."

Lyla laughed softly as she managed to reach the door to lock it behind Pippa as she left.

Pippa stood in the corridor for a moment. "What a strange twist of fate. A man and a cause. I needed something in my life, and I found double."

Her smile mocked her wish for a change in the even tempo of her existence of late. "Next time around I'll be more specific in my wishing."

CHAPTER SEVEN

"I beg your pardon?" Pippa questioned in a throaty whisper.

Tony shot her a look, trying to analyze the expression on her face. Despite the fact that he had a very pretty fiancé, it was difficult not to allow his eyes to wander to the ivory flesh superbly displayed in the scarlet gown. The dress was backless, sleeveless, and skin-taut to the hips, where it flared without a gather to the floor. No ornament adorned the fabric. The diamonds in Pippa's ears and around her neck made any other decoration superfluous.

"The Luck brothers have asked if you would sit with them tonight," he repeated carefully. "Since you seemed to be friends, I changed the seating."

Pippa tapped her forefinger to her lips, staring across the linen draped tables that were quickly filling with her fellow passengers. She was looking for one special face. An instant later she found it. Joshua met her eyes across the distance. Even from where she stood, she could read the challenge in his glance and the lift of his brow.

A perfect move, she congratulated him silently. Assurance would have made her angry. Arrogance would have turned her off, and awe-struck admiration would have been a boring repetition of others who had chased and lost her.

His strength against her own. A volatile mix, a recipe for destruction or creation. Her look whispered her thoughts across the room. The slow inclination of his head brought a smile. This trip was very interesting indeed.

"If there is a problem..." Tony offered hesitantly.

Pippa focused on his anxious frown, her lips curving gently. "Don't worry about it. I quite like the arrangement," she murmured.

His face cleared immediately, his grin sparkling with relief. "Next time, I'll make sure I check with you personally," he promised.

"It would be best," she agreed.

"I'll take you to your table."

She touched his arm, stopping him. "Unnecessary. I know the way." She glanced briefly over her shoulder to the others waiting for his assistance.

"You're busy."

Tony looked at her for a moment, then nodded before turning to the next passenger waiting in line. Pippa ignored the activity around her, the male eyes that marked her progress, the female ones that envied her poise and beauty.

Her eyes on Joshua. she moved through the maze of tables, her body swaying with a dancer's elegance with every twist and turn. Because she watched him so carefully, she knew the moment interest fused with desire. Her own blood heated, her lashes fanning down just so to increase the effect.

The chase was champagne and fire. She had played the game before, occasionally even to its conclusion, but it had never been this intense.

She stopped in front of his table, looking through half-closed eyes as he rose and pulled out her chair.

"You do that well," Josh murmured, bending next to her ear as he seated her.

Pippa laughed deep in her throat, tilting her head back ever so slightly. His lips were tantalizingly close. She ignored the temptation. "I am no innocent."

Josh took the chair across from hers, studying her face, finding it impossible to read. "Is that supposed to put me off?"

"Hardly." She picked up the water glass, rotating it gently in her palms before taking a slow sip. "I just want to make sure we understand each other. I never play unless I'm very sure what the stakes are and which game. You set this up."

Her arm moved in a graceful arc. "I don't think you're a man who does anything on the spur of the moment. Therefore, you have a purpose, a goal. I am no man's trophy."

Josh sat back, startled at the facts being delivered in that bedroom drawl that was becoming intimately familiar. "I look like a trophy hunter to you?" he asked, oddly flattered she would be wary of him. This was from a man who dished out relaxing and pleasant sex. Not bad.

Pippa studied the grin tugging at the corners of his mouth. The humor glinting in his eyes appealed to her. "This voyage is doing you good," she replied, deciding that evading his question was a better tactic for the moment.

Josh didn't blink at the quick change. "It's definitely different. It started with a strange plane ride and went on from there."

She laughed huskily. "You looked so impossibly disapproving. That kind of thing always brings out the worst in me."

Pippa shrugged and Joshua watched in fascination as the scarlet dress shifted and didn't lose its precarious embrace of her curves.

"Do you own anything that doesn't require glue to keep it in place?"

Pippa's eyes danced at the curious question. She looked down at her breasts. "Well, not really. I don't like clothes much. Too constricting by a half. And I believe in ecology."

This time he did blink. "What does one have to do with the other?"

"Less fabric, less trees, plants, chemicals, or whatever. Less pollution and less use of our resources."

The waiter arrived to take their order. Neither took much time deciding, almost as though both were eager to get back to the thrust and parry of the conversation.

"You have a unique point of view."

"But I am unique. All of us are, regardless of how we try to hide it or deny it. The difference is that I don't pretend mediocrity unless it exists."

Intrigued, he leaned forward slightly. "I can't believe you're mediocre at anything."

She chuckled. "Actually, I am. Can't cook worth beans. With the notable exception of pancakes. Those are the best in the world, a consumer's opinion, not my own. I also have a running feud with anything high tech, and early clutter is my favorite form of decorating."

"Writing probably makes those kinds of things impossible to pursue."

She angled her head, analyzing his expression. "Making excuses for me?"

"I think I am," he agreed after a second's reflection. "Odd."

"Do you ever make them for yourself?"

"No." His reply was immediate, abrupt, almost angry.

"And for your brother?"

He drew back, suddenly wary. "How did he get into this?"

"My writer's personality coming through. You two look awkward with each other in spite of the fact you both seem to be trying to reach out." She picked up her wineglass, sipping at the dry white as she watched him.

"I don't think this kind of questioning is in any game either of us knows," Josh said slowly, cold determination blotting out the warmth.

Pippa accepted the reprimand, silently cursing the sudden and subtle change in her focus with this man. She was asking the kind of things and seeing too deeply for a woman who wasn't interested in long-term commitments.

She raised her glass, her lips creating a smile that didn't reach her eyes. "Touché, my cautious companion. For a moment, I forgot the moves. No commitment. No depth. Just pleasure."

Josh frowned, uneasy with the description, although it would have been his own. Before he could comment, Pippa headed the conversation into safer territory, asking about his business. By the time dinner was over. Josh had given more information about himself than he had realized existed while he was no closer to understanding Pippa than he had been at the beginning of the evening.

"Do you do that deliberately?"

Pippa glanced at him, her brows raised as though she hadn't caught his meaning. "What?"

"Change personalities."

"Occasionally, out of necessity." Her shoulders shifted, changing the light reflection in the diamonds she wore. Their fire paled in comparison to the brightness of her eyes.

"Always keep the opposition guessing?"

"Something like that."

"Sorry I'm late," Joe announced as he arrived at the table. Pippa sat back in her chair, at ease with the interruption. Josh looked anything but pleased, she noted.

"You missed dinner," Josh said, signaling for the waiter.

"I'm not that hungry. Not now at least."

Josh gave him a sharp look, seeing remnants of something he didn't recognize in his eyes. "Problems?"

Joe shook his head. "Not the kind you mean. It takes a while for me to unwind sometimes. I'll be all right."

He looked at Pippa. "So, what did I miss?"

"Not World War Three," she returned dryly. "Stop looking so eager."

"Well, you have to admit neither of you is particularly retiring. I thought I would find you squared off with skewers at five paces."

"Mr. Luck?" Both men turned as the waiter stopped beside their table.

"Which one?" Josh asked.

The man looked startled then replied, "Joshua Luck."

"Yes?"

"A call for you, sir. A Ms. Evans."

Josh rose, frowning. "That's my office with an emergency. I'll see you later." Without waiting for a reply, he strode away.

Joe glanced at Pippa, expecting irritation if not outright anger at the way his brother had dismissed her so abruptly.

"You aren't annoyed," he said, surprised.

Pippa picked up her wine. "Should I be? Your brother lives for his work. No woman takes the place of that for him, especially not a stranger that he is attracted to but wishes he wasn't."

"You're very candid."

"There is no reason not to be."

Joe looked down at his hands then up into eyes that seemed to somehow be kind in a woman he would have said had little of the generally accepted definition of kindness. He had no right to do what he was about to do. Perhaps, it was his conscience about a past over which he had had no control. Perhaps, it was a debt he felt he owed, but he had to take the risk.

"Whatever is between you, don't hurt him. He's been hurt enough."

"He wouldn't thank you for seeing that," Pippa murmured.

"No." Joe's eyes, so like Josh's, sharpened. "How did you know?"

"I could plead paranormal abilities, but the truth is that I have a nephew who could be a younger version of your brother. Both self-contained men often cold, brittle, ruthless, heartless."

Joe's arm sliced the air in a negative gesture.

"That's a damn lie."

"You and I know that, but most of the world sees them that way and they see themselves that way. It's safer."

"Damn, are you part witch?" The second he asked the question he knew the real answer. "No, you know because you are the same under all of that."

"The camouflage is different."

"What happens now?"

"You should know that the future is written in the past. Read it there. Josh told me at dinner he came on a whim. He wanted to recreate a tie between you.

I, too, came on a whim, a need to break out of the predictability that my life has become. The wheels are set in motion. Neither of us is immune to the other and both of us are wary of anything beyond the most superficial of relationships.

If either of us was stronger, or less vulnerable to change right now, we would walk away. As it is, the game will be played. Nothing can stop the passage of one moment into the next."

Joe stared at her, stunned speechless by the expressionless tone of her voice. The accent, the husky, sensual drawl was missing. Missing, too, was the gleam of humor, of curiosity that had lurked in her eyes before.

This woman was strong, a fighter, a cynic, a saint, and a sinner. A believer in creation and yet a fatalist, too. A strange and dangerously beautiful combination of traits. As every man before him, Joe was caught by her power and entranced by her rarity. Even as he saw her virtues, he touched her weakness, her need to be accepted.

He reached out. Her hand met his. Her eyes were fearless, bold, and clear as they locked with his. He offered silently the gift that had not been sought. Her head moved gently, a slight but unmistakable nod of ascent.

He closed his eyes, better to block the sound of the world beyond the seclusion of their place in the shadows of the great dining room. "You will begin a new phase. The design of the future lies not in your hands, but your hands control the picture that will be made. Be careful of your choices. The sweeter the reward, the more bitter the bait."

Pippa let the words sink into her mind, knowing a true gift of foreknowledge when she felt it. Joseph Luck was all he was reported to be and more. Though the prophesy was a cryptic exercise, she sensed its truth.

"Thank you," she said simply.

He shook his head, trying to clear away the traces of pain the next few days would bring them all. For in seeing Pippa's future, he had touched Josh and himself. For the first time in his adult life, he almost wished he did not see beyond the moment.

"If I did not know what must come cannot be stopped, I would wish you away from here. You are the catalyst that will either bring us all to our knees or lift us beyond ourselves."

Pippa drew her hand from his, suddenly unutterably weary. She rose, looking down at him for a moment longer.

"I learned a long time ago that running is totally useless. But like you, I wish that I had not come to this place and time." Without another word she turned and walked silently through the crowded room.

Joe watched her go, admiring her strength even as he feared it. "Joshua, you don't know this woman at all. None of us do," he whispered.

Joshua slammed the lid on his briefcase, angered that this trip had been interrupted. A few calls, a slight change in wording on a contract and the assistance of his very capable secretary had made for a speedy resolution that didn't necessitate him leaving the ship.

For the first time in his life, he didn't want his business to have top priority and that angered him even more. Changing values in midlife was a bit like changing cars in the middle of rush hour traffic on the interstate. Damn risky and life-threatening.

He stalked to the bar and poured himself a drink. He took a hefty swallow, his eyes fastened on the porthole and the black velvet sky it framed. Joe and Pippa were out there. What were they talking about, thinking?

He didn't understand either of them, yet they mattered to him. He could understand Joe's pull on his emotions, but Pippa was a different story. And it was no good telling himself that sex was his single motive. He had never been a liar to anyone, least of all himself.

"If I had any sense, I would forget I ever saw the woman," he muttered.

CHAPTER EIGHT

"If I had any sense, I would forget I ever saw that man," Pippa mumbled, staring at her reflection. "Every time I touch him, I stumble into that damn wanting again. Things are getting out of control, and I can't back down."

She thought of Joe's words. Maybe it wasn't too late. Maybe this one time it would be better to run than to face the future. Maybe next time she would be better prepared to handle herself.

The moment the thought was born she knew she would never be able to live with herself if she walked away. She would always wonder what she had missed and, besides, there was more to consider than just her needs.

There was Lyla. She could not desert the younger woman now. Lyla was too lost, too alone, too hurt to handle any more pain. Pippa lifted her head and faced her reflection. She would meet tomorrow as she always had, head on.

The next morning brought no change in her thinking. Pippa showered and slipped into a pair of rose crinkle-cotton slacks and lightweight, wide-necked blouse. The deep scoop and sleeveless style was cool and brief. After twisting her hair into a rope around her head, she added a pair of long, gold glitzy hoops to her ears. The effect was resort flashy, and fun.

She smiled, giving her hips an extra swing as she left her stateroom. Now all she had to do was roust Lyla out of bed, arrange for Joe and Josh to escort them into town, and coerce Lyla into shedding her plain brown wrapper. The day was full of promise she decided as she knocked on Lyla's door.

"Come in," Lyla called, grimacing as the sound of her own voice rattled in her head. Putting a hand over her eyes, she waited for the pounding to stop. She never overindulged.

"Bad head?" Pippa asked, coming over to the couch to survey the scene of moderate debauchery.

Lyla opened one eye and tried to glare. The effect was little more than an irritated squint. Pippa chuckled and moved to the phone to summon a steward.

"Go take a shower. I know a trick or two to get you vertical."

"I don't want to be vertical," Lyla announced positively. "It was hard enough to stumble out of bed and get to this couch. I was going to order breakfast, but my stomach started rolling in a way that made me change my mind."

Pippa ignored the small show of temper. "Sure you don't want to be vertical? You can't possibly intend to spend the next thirteen days hiding in the shadows and missing the sights. There are some gorgeous men on this boat..."

"Ship..." Lyla corrected automatically.

"Whatever." Pippa shrugged. The gesture made the blouse slip lower.

Lyla sighed. "Pippa, I know you're trying to help, but I can't face anyone yet. I certainly don't want to meet any men."

"Sure you do. Every single woman does if she's telling the truth. Besides, I think you'll like who I have picked out for you."

Lyla paused in the act of pushing herself off the couch. "Out for me? What do you mean by that?"

"His name is Joseph Luck and he's one of the psychics on board. Tall, delicious body, and eyes that make you think you can tell him anything and he won't condemn you."

Pippa closed the distance separating them, stopping only a step away. Her expression no longer showed humor, rather gravity that only her family and Josh had ever seen.

"I know our acquaintance is short and there isn't one damn reason why, especially with your history, that you should trust me. But I really wish you would. I won't hurt you. Neither will Joe. It's not in his nature. Let him and us brighten the next few days for you. Relax and play with us. You won't regret it, I promise."

Lyla stared into her eyes, caught by the plea and the strength that seemed to flow out of this woman in an unending wave. Hope, the human commodity that had been bankrupt in her soul for so long, found its first deposit. The headache that had been nagging at her mind eased. Without realizing it, the tension about going out in public that had dogged her footsteps through the hell of the last four years lost some of its edge.

"All right," she said slowly.

Pippa rewarded her courage with a smile and a nod. She had planned to stay while Lyla had breakfast and changed. Instead, she decided to leave while she had Lyla's agreement. Less chance for Lyla to change of her mind.

"Now, find something, anything, in that infamous case of yours that isn't brown. Order something to eat while you are at it. You didn't have dinner last night and nothing so far this morning. You don't want to be passing out from hunger. An hour should be enough time. I'll meet you on deck by the gang plank."

"You aren't staying?"

"Have things to do." She headed for the door, wishing she had thought to call Joe before she had left her cabin. She could only hope he was still in his stateroom. It was imperative she talk to him before he met Lyla.

"Pippa?"

Pippa glanced over her shoulder.

"Thanks."

"I haven't done anything yet."

"You've done the best thing of all. You've been my friend. I won't forget."

Pippa laughed softly. "I'll hold you to that when you're ready to wring my neck."

Lyla shook her head, not prepared to joke. It had been so long since anyone had believed in her or cared about her. "That day will never come. "

"Oh, it will. It always does. That's another promise I'll make you."

Lyla grinned, feeling just a little lighter than she had the day before. "Want to bet?"

"Sure, but we'll have to come up with some really inventive stakes. I don't go in for the mundane."

This time Lyla laughed, her humor soft, free. "I can tell that." She nodded toward the bright outfit. "You might want to pull up that blouse, before you give some man a heart attack."

Pippa scowled, her eyes dancing with amusement. "But, Lyla, my friend, that's just what I intend doing," she replied wickedly as she sauntered out the door.

She could hear Lyla chuckling as she closed the panel. The minute Pippa could no longer be seen, her expression changed. Purpose replaced the teasing light in her eyes. She had to find Joe. Luck, in more ways than one, was with her. Joe was in his stateroom, alone.

"I have to talk to you," she announced the moment he opened the door.

Frowning at the urgency in her voice, Joe gestured her inside. "Problem with Josh?"

"No. This one is for you."

Startled, he said, "Me? How?"

"I need your help with a woman."

Joe froze in mid step, staring at her. "I beg your pardon." For the life of him he couldn't think of a possible explanation for her words.

"Oh, sit down. You're giving me a crick in my neck, and I don't have much time. Are both you Lucks so wary that a simple request should be so impossible? Use that extra sensory input you've got and think."

Joe sat. Short as his exposure had been to Pippa, he had learned that nothing she did was quite what he expected.

"All right. I'm listening."

"I'll tell you up front, I'm breaking a confidence. If I didn't believe you're closed as a clam, I wouldn't be doing it."

His interest caught, Joe prompted, "All right. If you need it, you have my promise that whatever you tell me won't go beyond this point."

Pippa studied him for a moment, praying her instinct for the truth in people wouldn't let her down for the first time in her life. More than just Lyla's enjoyment of the trip rested in this man's hands.

"There is a woman on this ship, Lyla Carson."

Joe's frown deepened as the familiarity of the name made itself felt. He couldn't quite place how yet.

"Before you start searching your memory, I'll tell you that she's made the headlines here in Florida. She was involved in a drug sting about four years ago. Initially, she was the one arrested. The media crucified her, and her friends and family deserted her."

Her internet research after she had returned to her suite last night had filled in some ugly blanks in Lyla's story.

"She wasn't guilty. If there hadn't been a stubborn investigator on the case, she probably would have been tried and convicted instead of ending up as a star witness for the prosecution. The trial finished the day the ship sailed. She walked right out of the courtroom, got into a taxi, and got on board."

"And somehow walked straight into you," he guessed.

"I've always attracted challenges. A human lightning rod of sorts."

His lips curved slightly, but he stayed focused on the main topic. "So, what do you want from me?"

"First of all, do you have anything on your work schedule this morning."

"Not until early afternoon, two if you need an exact hour."

"How about plans with your brother?"

"We were thinking of going into town to look around. Flexible on the time to start. I've been waiting for him to contact me."

"Great. Just what I need. How do you feel about making up a party?"

"With this woman you are talking about?"

She nodded. "Yes. She needs help, Joe. Nothing huge to you or me but being out with people who don't believe she is guilty is something she hasn't experienced in years. Doing simple things like shopping a little, sightseeing."

"Have you talked to Josh about this?"

"I haven't seen him since he left the table last night." She studied him for a moment. "You think he would object?"

He sighed deeply. "Not object exactly. Just not his usual way with outsiders."

"I wouldn't call Lyla's situation normal for any of us. The media crucified her. Even with someone else being convicted there are still going to be people who will wonder or even outright believe she was a willing participant."

He nodded, his face grim. "The public often judges too quickly and gives the benefit of the doubt so slowly."

"Will you help me get her into town and into some shops for clothes, something besides the fade-into-the-woodwork garbage she's wearing now. To bolster her confidence. Help get that damn empty look out of her eyes. No being deserves to see no hope in the future. That's a hell that even Satan himself can't rival."

Joe had his share and more of the hopeless, those who had been kicked by life too many times to want to step out of what tiny comfort zone they still possessed. He could no more refuse Pippa's plea than he could refuse to take his next breath.

"This should be interesting."

Pippa smiled faintly. "You're thinking of Josh. I think he may surprise you."

"He may surprise you too. You haven't seen him in his real world. He is not a person who reaches out emotionally. Our father was a cold man, and our mother didn't stand up to him. He did everything he could to mold Josh into the man like himself. He didn't manage to completely turn Josh as cold as he was, but Josh doesn't let his emotions have much impact in his life."

"I'm not asking him for anything but a few hours of sightseeing and lunch. He can always say no."

"If he does, it's going to be his loss. Just don't be surprised if he does refuse."

"I won't be," she said ambiguously. Pippa rose to leave.

Joe followed, sensing something beneath the obvious purpose of her visit. "What is it you're not telling me?"

With the advantage of her back to him. Pippa had a second to school her features to calm. "I don't know what you're talking about."

"You do. But you're blocking me somehow." He studied her intently. "Are you sure you aren't psychic?"

"I thought everyone had that capability."

"You're evading the question."

"I don't practice if that is what you mean."

"You know it isn't."

Pippa glanced at the door. "I have to go. I need to talk to Josh before I meet Lyla. If Lyla gets on deck and doesn't find me waiting for her, she'll retreat to her stateroom again and I'll have to pry her out with a crowbar."

"Pippa, I don't like tricks any more than Josh does."

Pippa looked back at him. "I don't play tricks. I never have."

Joe felt her sincerity, recognized the truth when he heard it. Surprised at the error he had made on something so simple, he didn't pursue the next level of possibility. Instead, he smiled slightly.

"I guess I'm more wary than I thought."

"It's a good defense," she murmured, before leaving him.

She headed for Josh's cabin, hoping he was still there and not wandering the ship. She didn't have time for hide-and-seek to find him before she met Lyla.

She knocked on his door, mentally crossing her fingers for luck.

"Joe, I," Josh began as he opened the door.

"Not Joe although I just left him. There has been a slight change of plans for this morning." She stepped forward.

Josh studied her for a second then moved aside to let her into his suite. The night's sleep had brought no answers about the woman standing in front of him.

Purpose radiated from her in a silent demand he do something. What had yet to be determined. He could always say no he assured himself.

"What kind of change of plans?"

"You are getting two more added to your party going ashore," she announced with a grin. "Lyla and I are invited."

"Drop the other shoe, starting with who invited you." He tucked his hands in his pockets and waited. The anticipation in Pippa's eyes held a distinct element of challenge.

"I had a feeling you weren't going to be chivalrous about including us."

She made herself comfortable on the arm of the sofa since he didn't look as though he was going to suggest they sit to talk.

"Does chivalry still exist these days?"

"It does in my world, and I hope, for today, it does in yours." She watched his face and could see nothing in his expression to give her clue to his reaction. "Lyla needs help, badly needs help."

He frowned. "Who is Lyla and what kind of help?"

Pippa glanced toward the small desk near the floor to ceiling glass that gave a wonderful view of the shore and the town that was waiting to be explored. An open laptop sat ready for input or research.

"Can I use you lap for a moment." She nodded toward the computer.

"For what?"

The suspicion in his voice was almost a duplicate of the suspicion when she had first introduced herself on the plane.

"Not to steal any business secrets. I want to show you something and I don't have a lot of time." She rose and took the few steps needed to reach the keyboard.

Aware Joshua was watching her every move, Pippa typed Lyla's name into the search bar and hit enter. In seconds, she had the latest information on the case in which Lyla had been a major player.

"This is why. I can give you the highlights, or you can read it for yourself."

Curiosity had ever been a trait he had tried to tame. He read the data swiftly, frowning when the charges had been brought against Lyla then dropped when the real culprit had been found.

His expression darkened as he absorbed the years it had taken to mount the investigation and secure the source of the drug connection. The trial had been lengthy and ugly with Lyla's name mired by innuendo and misinformation as often as facts and truth.

There were pictures of Lyla as a professional with a reputation for fast tracking her career. She looked sleek, elegant and in control. As the months of investigation and false charges became years, she had lost weight and that striking presence in such a way that it was almost impossible to believe the transformation.

"What exactly are you thinking, Pippa? What possible good is having the four of us sightsee together?"

"One, two attractive men escorting two dynamite women around this morning. Two, Lyla needs clothes that she doesn't have. Brown is not a good color on her. Three, a hair cut that works for her face shape if I can manage to find a stylist in the hours we have."

"You know damn well this ship has a salon, boutiques that offer everything from the skin out and all the accessories that any woman could want. Not to mention a spa, cosmetics from many of the high-end companies. Lyla doesn't have to leave the ship to get a makeover."

"Only a man would be so literal. Yes, she could do it here in the full view of the passengers she is surrounded by for the next thirteen days. Do you think a stylist is going to be able to resist bragging about the new look he or she created for Lyla? Or the clothes salesperson who helps Lyla become a swan instead of a drab bird? She's had enough of that kind of scrutiny."

He was dressed as casually as she was in a blue pullover short sleeved shirt and light tan slacks. Pippa laid her hand on his bare arm. His skin was warm, the muscles beneath her fingers firm.

"She needs friends, Joshua. Someone who doesn't look at her and wonder if she is really innocent. Joe agreed to come. I'll take care of the shopping part and you two can enjoy yourselves without us for a while."

Josh raked his fingers through his hair. This trip wasn't turning out to be like anything he had imagined. His only goal had been to make a bridge of some kind between himself and his brother, his only remaining living relative.

"I think this is a crazy idea but I will go along with it. This time," he warned.

Pippa breathed a mental sigh of relief. The first two phases were complete. She glanced at her watch. "Ten minutes. We are meeting at the gangplank."

"She didn't even say thank you," Josh muttered as she zipped out the door, closing it smartly behind her. "I should have said no. Why the hell didn't I?"

He knew why. That crazy woman appealed to him in a way no other woman ever had. How did he say no to Pippa when she was so determined to help a stranger who had gotten kicked in the teeth so many times that she had lost herself along the way?

That kind of heart, that kind of caring was so rare that he had never encountered it before. In his world favors were done for gain and profit. Pippa stood to get nothing in return that he could see.

CHAPTER NINE

Joshua watched stop to Pippa lean against the rail. There was no sign of Lyla yet. Pippa seemed deep in thought, blind to the controlled madness around her.

His gaze slipped over the cotton outfit she was barely wearing. As usual, more than a little skin was on display. Her walk had been an invitation to the men she passed, but she had seemed unaware of the stir she had caused. That glorious hair was a bright crown, catching the sunlight, trapping it as though the light was a source of energy.

"She has a way of holding attention even when she is standing still," Joe murmured, watching his brother's changing expression and remembering the woman who had reached out to another woman in comfort, caring, and solace. The more he knew of Pippa, the more he liked her.

"Too much attention. I haven't decided whether it's deliberate or natural. Any man who was interested in her would constantly be fighting off her admirers."

He stiffened as a young surfer type stopped beside Pippa, going so far as to put his hand on her arm. Without realizing it, Josh took a step forward.

Joe stifled a small grin. Unless he was very much mistaken, his brother's days of being the controlled executive who could quell a board full of dissenters with a look were numbered.

"I don't think it would be wise to start a fight here," he said dryly.

"Look at her. Why doesn't she shake that skinny puppy loose? He isn't even fully grown."

"From the looks of it, I'd say that's just what she's trying to do."

Josh shifted his shoulders. Something about shedding his normal attire for resort wear had changed his emotions. He felt freer, more capable of giving in to urges. Right now, the urge to rearrange that amorous twit's face was almost irresistible.

"I think it's time I'll keep Pippa company while we wait for Lyla," he muttered.

Joe trailed him. "I think I'll join you."

"I don't need any help," Josh threw over his shoulder.

Joe grinned openly. "I didn't think you did. But your target might." He glanced significantly at Josh's tightly curled fists.

Josh looked down, making a conscious effort to relax. Pippa was probably more than capable of taking care of herself. He had a strong suspicion he was making a fool of himself. He started to turn away.

At that moment, the breeze shifted, carrying Pippa's voice clearly to him.

"I'm fine. Really. I don't need a guide."

"But I insist. This place is much more fun for a woman like you with a man to show her around."

Pippa studied the college boy in front of her, beginning to get annoyed at his persistence and the way he was ogling her. She doubted the kid had ever heard the words discretion and finesse. She'd try tact one more time and then the gloves would be off if he didn't take the hint.

"I'm waiting for someone," she insisted firmly.

"That old dude doesn't deserve you." He nodded at Josh who was clearly coming closer. "You're too young and..."

"I'd leave unsaid the rest of what Pippa is," Josh advised, coming up behind Pippa.

Pippa swung around, straight into Josh's arms.

Before she could recover, be pulled her closer and dropped a kiss on her lips as she raised her head.

"Sorry, I took so long, honey. The office is driving me nuts trying to iron out the details of that mall deal." He glared at the surfer. "You still here?"

This man could kiss as no other. It was daylight, with a score of people milling about them, Joe overlooking the scene, an erstwhile suitor glaring in the background and all she wanted to do was get closer.

"I was talking to her," the boy said angrily. "So why don't you butt out?"

Pippa froze at the challenge thrown between the two men. She felt Josh tense. She touched his cheek, smiling into his furious eyes.

"Darling, I'd prefer that you not tear him apart. Remember the last nice young man you put in the hospital."

Josh took his eyes from the boy to stare at Pippa in amazement. "Darling?" he questioned blankly.

She batted her lashes at him before turning in his arms to confront the source of the problem.

"We had a fight."

She shrugged, her blouse starting to slide off one shoulder. Before it could reach the point of no return, Josh caught the fabric, his fingers smoothing it back in place.

The surfer followed the progressive movement of Josh's hand, his expression changing with the gesture. His body relaxed as he shook his head.

"Man, you got your work cut out for you. Glad she's yours and not mine." Turning quickly, he left them.

Pippa scowled at his retreating back. "Well, I like that. Of all the rotten things to say."

Josh pulled her back against his chest and leaned his chin on her bright hair. "Honey, the kid knows big trouble when he sees it." He pulled the edge of her blouse higher, frowning at the scanty cut. "Who the devil buys your clothes?"

"I do," she said sweetly, shrugging out of his hold and yanking the off the shoulder design back in place. "This is cool, non-crease..."

"And nearly not there," Josh interrupted bluntly. "A woman your age..."

Pippa drew herself up in outrage. At least three men stopped in shock at the centerfold look to her figure. Only Josh and Joe noticed the sudden interest they were attracting.

"You've done it now," Joe muttered, glaring at their audience. Josh was too busy scowling at the star of the show.

"Just what do you mean about a woman of my age?"

"Haven't you ever heard of understatement?"

"Yes, and it's boring," she snapped, propping her hands on her hips.

The effect was all the more devastating. Joe turned so that he was blocking most of the scene. Josh hauled Pippa into his arms. An error, for Pippa was no woman to be hauled anywhere. She was wearing soft canvas shoes, but she made the most of a toned body and leverage, delivering a swift kick in the center of his shin.

Josh barely managed to swallow an oath at the pain. His hands tightened on her skin. "Do that one more time and I'll toss you over my shoulder like the baggage you are."

Pippa blew the hair that had fallen over her brow out of her eyes. Her eyes glittered with temper. Desire had never been farther from her mind.

"I knew you were trouble last night," she muttered, bracing her hands against his chest.

"It takes one to know one," Josh retaliated, watching her and her feet. Only a fool trusted a growing storm.

"You two settle this now. I am not standing here all day," Joe commanded, doing his best to look as if acting as a human shield was as natural as breathing.

"Shut up." The two voices with almost the same inflection spoke at once.

"Don't tell my brother to shut up."

"You did."

"That's different."

Joe rolled his eyes, torn between laughing and wanting to shake them both. "This is not helping my image."

Josh's scowl deepened. Pippa's glare sharpened. Silence reigned for all of twenty seconds.

"I am not baggage," Pippa said finally.

Josh shook his head, a grin tugging at the corners of his lips. "You are, too."

He dropped a kiss on her mouth as he felt her foot lift for the next strike. "If you kick me again, I'll turn you over my knee right here in front of everyone who cares to look."

Pippa froze in midmotion. That tone wasn't a bluff. Those eyes, despite the humor lurking in the dark depths, were filled with purpose.

For the first time in her life, Pippa considered someone else's strength against her own. Backing down before had always meant losing ground. But suddenly she wondered if this time there wasn't more to be gained than lost. Slowly, watching him closely, she lowered her foot.

His smile was admiration and respect, a salute rather than an expression of triumph. It was then that Pippa knew her decision for the immediate future was made. She smiled back, her body softening in his arms.

"Well, what next?" she asked huskily.

Josh glanced from her face to the gangplank connecting the ship to the dock. The stream of people disembarking was noisy.

"Sightseeing?"

He looked at her, one brow cocked. His mind had a number of other far more delightful possibilities, but years of habit were hard to unlearn in a few days. Besides, pouncing on Pippa was a risky venture. The woman had a quick tongue and very fast feet.

"Sounds wonderful. And shopping. But..."

His eyes narrowed at the tone that was more a husky drawl. When Pippa turned up the heat he had learned to look out.

"Am I going to like this?" he demanded.

Before Pippa could reply, Lyla approached the group.

Focusing more on Pippa than the two handsome men standing guard over her, Lyla murmured, "Pippa?"

Pippa turned, smiling. "You're just in time. Joe is the quiet one and the one looking like he's ready to strangle me is Josh. They're taking us shopping and sightseeing for the day." She looked over her shoulder.

Josh had his comments ready, but one look at Pippa's steel-eyed determination and he swallowed them. A second glance at the woman standing before them who looked as if she couldn't decide whether to stay or flee touched some long-forgotten core of compassion.

He angled his head, watching his brother. He found Joe smiling gently at Lyla, clearly waiting for Lyla's reaction to Pippa's arrangement.

"Shopping sounds good if I don't have to plow in and out of every tourist trap in George Town," he said going along with the plan that Pippa had concocted. He looked down at the woman still in his arms. Her smile told him he had chosen the right tone.

Pippa slipped out his hold. She could see Lyla was far from comfortable with the male addition to the expedition. She hooked her arm through Lyla's.

"Joe has been here a number of times since he has done this cruise presentation before. I thought he would be a great guide for us."

Joe could see what had drawn Pippa to Lyla. She wore the damage that the past had done to her like an invisible cloak. Its heavy folds were draining the life from her.

"Actually, this is my fifth cruise. Since I like exploring, I've found a number of great local shops and restaurants."

"I don't want to put you to the trouble...."

If he couldn't beat them, he had to join them, Josh decided since Joe added his weight to Pippa's. "I like the idea of skipping the tourist haunts."

"I rented us a horse drawn carriage." Joe gestured with a wave of his hand to the almost empty gangplank. Various conveyances were filling with eager passengers intent on enjoying the day. A single carriage waited a little beyond the other modes of transport.

"Everyone ready?"

From their elevated position, Lyla could see the white open carriage and the gray horse waiting so patiently for them. Their kindness, Pippa and two men she had just met, touched her deeply. Her eyes stung with tears she refused to shed. They had gone to so much trouble for her.

"Thank you all."

Pippa squeezed her arm then laughed gaily. "Honey, you haven't seen anything yet. I intend to shop until I drop and so are you."

"I am going to be relaxing with a drink in my hand while you do it," Josh reminded her firmly. "I do not want to hear 'how do I look' from either of you. I am a neutral party, and I am staying a neutral party."

Pippa urged Lyla down the plank. "The day I ask a man how I look in something is the day I decide I have lost every brain cell I possess as well as my sanity," Pippa shot back.

Somehow, Josh still wasn't sure how two hours later, Pippa had managed to pair Joe with Lyla for the hair styling and wardrobe detail with the two of them as the spectators.

Pippa sat in the peacock back wicker chair. Lyla, at the moment, was trying on a number of outfits that she and Joe had persuaded her were just the thing for a cruise. The day was progressing just as she had hoped.

Joe was playing judge allowing her to retreat with Josh to the small alcove by the front window of the boutique. Sunlight streamed into the shop, touching the island decor with gold and creating flashes of light on the mirrors and faux jewelry.

"I told you this would work," Pippa said. She smiled with she heard Lyla laugh at something Joe said.

"Getting Lyla outfitted like the attractive young woman she is, definitely," he replied with a nod toward the carriage that waited in the shade of the tree across the street from the shop. The stack of bags and packages were clearly visible in the small cargo area at the back.

"You didn't mention a thing about pairing her up with Joe."

"I didn't pair them up exactly."

"Right. Two carriage seats. Joe and Lyla on one. You and I on the other."

Pippa took a sip of her coconut flavored drink. The citrus mix added a zing to the concoction. She should have asked the name, but she liked the mystery too much to bother with knowing what she was drinking.

"I could have sat with Joe if you prefer Lyla."

Josh was too experienced not to catch the provocation in her look and her tone. At another time he would have taken her up on the tone. Right now, he had more to worry about than his attraction to this maddening woman.

Josh sighed deeply. "I'm concerned about the way Joe seems to be taken with Lyla. I don't understand your angle in this."

"Do I have to have one?"

"So far I haven't seen you do anything without a reason. Logic would expand that to this situation as well."

He didn't want to believe her capable of some hidden purpose, but she didn't seem the type given to altruistic impulses. He watched her intently, trying to read her expression.

Other than the faint flicker in her eyes that he could have sworn was hurt, he could find nothing to hold on to. Suddenly, obeying an impulse of his own, he leaned forward and took her hands in his.

"Tell me what's going on and I'll help you if I can."

On the one side, Josh had hurt and disappointed her, but with one touch he had soothed the pain and mitigated the disillusionment.

"She isn't guilty, Josh. You saw the research as well as I did. Everyone that kid has ever known turned against her, left her in the cruel light of the media and waited for her blood to flow to bathe in the gore.

She was so cut up that the simplest thing makes her want to hide. You're strong but think of what that media crucifixion that must have been like for her. She was twenty-four years old when it started. What were you doing at twenty-four?"

"Fighting for my independence from a man who didn't know the meaning of freedom," he answered without thought, her words touching a well deep inside him.

He remembered, too, the hopelessness of the situation, the need for change within the company that he had been unable to instigate from his junior position with the firm. He recalled the anger, the threats, the wish to tear his past and future to shreds and just run. But he hadn't. He had stayed, fought a losing battle, lost, and picked himself up to keep on fighting, growing tougher, surer, and more capable with every defeat until his father's passing.

He thought he had finally achieved a clear path to guide the failing company his sire had left behind. He had been wrong. Blindsided from the one person he had thought was on his side.

The ultimate betrayal of discovering Joe had worked against him in those terrible months after their parent's death had destroyed his trust, the bond they had shared and what was left of the only family he had.

"I could write a book about fighting the world alone," he murmured from the depths of his memories.

Pippa touched his cheek, watching his eyes, seeing his pain. "Then you should understand her. Stop thinking in facts and tally sheets. Look at her. A criminal wouldn't be crushed as she is. They wouldn't cringe as she has all morning, every time a stranger looks our way."

Josh gazed beyond her shoulder to the slender woman in the white shorts and pink shirt. The light caught the newly styled soft brown hair secured with a plastic clip similar to the one he had seen on Pippa. Her laugh was soft, low, and husky. She looked younger with every hour. She was pretty when she forgot her past.

He didn't miss the way Joe smiled at Lyla or his gentle teasing every time Lyla tried to fade in the background. He was the first one of them to get a smile. After only a few hours, Lyla looked to him when she was worried or uncomfortable.

"Joe likes to help. She is vulnerable. They could be badly hurt if one of them.... "

"They are adults, nudging at twenty-nine in Lyla's case." She lifted a brow.

"Joe's thirty-one."

"Your brother is more than capable of taking care of himself. Lyla is a lot stronger than even she knows, or she wouldn't be here right now," Pippa pointed out.

Josh studied Pippa closely. "I think you planned this," he said slowly.

The last carried no accusation, only a growing knowledge of her personality.

"I created an opportunity. What they do with it, is up to them." She waited, knowing that the truth had given Josh both a weapon and a shield. Which would he choose to use?

He hadn't expected her to admit to engineering the pairing of the two. What else was she expecting? More importantly, why? He lived in a world where everyone had an agenda. He rarely missed the markers, but he hadn't seen this one coming.

"You're a lethal woman, Pippa Weldon," he said, not sure whether it was admiration or frustration that drew the words from him. "I don't want him hurt, damn it. Her either. Have you thought of that?"

"Yes. Have you thought of what each could give the other? Lyla knows what your brother is and she accepts him completely. How often do you think that happens for him? With his talent, he is the one person who can know that she is truly innocent. How much do you think that means to her?

Look at them, Joshua. They both have shields, heavy duty armor. You would have to be blind not to see it. Joe is letting her close. She is opening to him. The walls are coming down for both of them."

Josh couldn't argue with the truth he could see with his own eyes. He reached for her hand, pulling her nearer.

"I don't know where any of us are heading. Nothing about this trip is going as planned. I hope you have a road map because I sure don't."

She leaned her head against his chest where his heart beat in time with hers. "I have a direction, but someone else is doing the driving. I won't know the way until we arrive."

He cupped the back of her neck, needing her close as he had rarely needed few things in his life. "I think I'm glad you picked me up, beautiful lady," he whispered as he leaned his chin on the silver crown of her hair. "I hope in the end all of us are glad to have touched you."

Pippa felt the sting of tears she never shed. Before she could stem the flow, they dampened his shirt.

Josh lifted her chin with his fingers, seeing the glistening traces on her cheeks. His smile was more tender than he knew. Pippa bathed in it, knowing then something she should have known from the second meeting.

Josh was a man she could love. Tough, aggressive, demanding, and just plain stubborn. He appealed to her senses, her heart, her mind, and her body. Remembering all the reasons why she wasn't made for commitment had never been harder.

"That's the nicest thing anyone has ever said to me," she whispered.

.

"I'm glad," he whispered back. "I want to live in your memory for a long time."

He could have added forever, but his newly awakened sensitivity told him that was the wrong word to use with this woman. "What do you say to a torrid thirteen-day affair?" he asked whimsically.

"I would love it," she replied promptly.

Whatever teasing that had gone into his and her reply died in the look they exchanged.

"Can we do it?" she murmured.

"Why not? We have no one to hurt and the time to give to ourselves."

"And survive?"

"We always have."

CHAPTER TEN

"I can't wear this," Lyla said warily.

She stared at the scantily clad length of her body. Her legs had never looked so long, her breasts so clearly defined. Even before the notoriety of the trial, her clothing tended to be restrained, more professional than feminine. With the white wrap skirt that completed the ensemble, there was more of her skin showing than was usual.

Joe shook his head, a smile tugging at his lips. His shoulders were braced against the edge of the long mirror, his hands tucked in the pockets of his white cotton pants.

"You've been saying the same thing to every outfit for the last hour."

Lyla glanced at him, startled. "Has it been that long? Why didn't you tell me?"

She looked over her shoulder to where Pippa and Josh sat by the window talking. She was horrified at the time she had taken with her indecisiveness.

"I didn't tell you because, until now, it didn't matter. However, I do have to get back to the ship soon for my presentation."

He studied her, liking the colorful outfit that she was determined not to buy. "Personally, I think this is the best choice yet. If you don't buy it, I will."

"You can't."

"Do you think I don't have the money?" His dark brows quirked at the thought. While he wasn't megawealthy, he only worked because he wanted to.

Lyla flushed, wishing she had never allowed Pippa to bully her into coming with her and the Luck brothers. Josh was quiet, speaking mostly to Pippa. She wasn't sure whether he approved of her or not. Joe watched her with eyes that saw too much.

"I never should have come," she muttered.

Before her lips closed around the last word, Joe pushed away from the wall and caught her shoulders. He shook her once, gently but firmly.

"Stop it, right now. You aren't guilty. Stop acting as if you were and are. You have a right to enjoy yourself and to look delicious in those shorts. You also have a right to smile just because something pleases you.

Don't let those fools who hurt you and turned away when you needed them the most, take any more from you. Stop looking down, trying to hide. Look up into the future. It's there waiting."

"You don't know what it's like."

His face hardened with his own memories of being shunned. "Don't I? Do you think you're the only one who has ever been ostracized by small-minded jackasses? You don't have the corner on pain. I've had my share. So has my brother and Pippa. Look at them!"

He turned her so that she had to see. "Really look. Pippa's style is flash and show. But is that the woman? Would that glitz have reached out to you if she hadn't seen below the surface? That kind of insight doesn't come by accident. It comes through knowledge and pain. And Josh, you think he judges you as the others do?"

"I never said that" she protested.

"No, you only avoid his eyes, shrink from being near him. Do you think we don't realize?" he demanded roughly. "Even if they didn't, I would. I spend my life at the mercy of the pain and emotion of those around me. Do you think I don't feel you and yours?"

Joe turned her back to him, searching her face for the life he could feel still smoldering in her. Her past had killed everything but that single bright flame of existence. Anger that he could hardly control filled him.

"Damn you, stop hiding," he commanded, just barely remembering to keep his voice down. "It wasn't your fault."

Suddenly it was as though someone had poked a giant hole in the wall of apathy that had surrounded her since the media had made public the real culprit in the drug ring. She had been so certain the worst was over, that if she was cleared of wrong doing, her life would return to normal.

How wrong she had been? The old adage, no smoke without fire had been a brand on her soul. Her friends and family hadn't really believed her total innocence. In some cases, they hadn't even tried to pretend she had been shown to have been a pawn in the scheme.

Anger to match Joe's rose, momentarily blotting out the need to cringe. She stiffened her spine. Her eyes flashed, the cloudy brown turning to bright amber with temper. The fire singed her cheeks with pink. Drawing herself up, she caught his wrists, twisted once, and freed herself.

"You have no right," she snapped, each word emerging clearly and starkly.

"Honey, you've been giving us the right all morning. Pippa, Josh, and I have been watching over you like three birds with one chick. It's been hard going, let me tell you."

He leaned back against the wall and folded his arms across his chest. Anger suited her far better than fear and shame. The tiny flame of life was turning into a bonfire of outrage. He could have shouted with triumph but settled for being an audience for now.

Lyla eyed the challenging pose and made her first decision. "Damn you all. You want me to strut around town in this getup, then I will. But the first idiot who makes a pass at me is going to get a straw handbag around his ears."

Joe laughed, his humor dark, rich, and thoroughly masculine. "As a weapon that isn't much of threat..."

Lyla had the totally uncharacteristic urge to stamp her foot. He was laughing at her, damn him. She took a step closer, eyeing him with no gentle intent.

"You want to be the first to try it?"

He cocked his head to one side. Her position gave him an excellent view of some decidedly feminine real estate. He could have been a gentleman and pointed that out, but he liked the scenery too much to give it up.

"Why not?" He reached out and pulled her into his arms. For the first time in his life, his emotions overshadowed all other considerations.

Lyla gasped, not really expecting him to take up the gauntlet. His lips covered hers before she could do more than mutter a half word. There, in front of anyone who cared to look, he kissed her deeply, his mouth taking its time with hers.

Before she could marshal her defenses, desire wrapped around her. Heat, his or hers, made a haven of the alcove that partially shielded them. Her hands crept up his shoulders, digging into the surprisingly firm muscles.

Joe lifted his head, his eyes fogged with passion, his breath hissing between his lips.

"Not one of my better impulses," he murmured, touching her face gently. He smiled crookedly. "You don't need a handbag with a kiss like that. You bring a man to his knees."

Lyla stared at him, suspecting he was teasing and discovering by his expression that he was not. Confidence in herself that she had lost began a slow climb back to self-assurance.

"Do I?" She stroked his cheek.

The real curiosity in her voice, the strange yearning look in her eyes, held Joe's attention. A hundred questions made a monkey mind out of his usual calm thoughts. But now was not the time or the place. With effort, he focused on the present and forced his needs back into the warmth of his memory.

"Now, will you buy this outfit?" he whispered.

She nodded slowly, suddenly deciding it wasn't so scanty after all. A woman who could bring a man to his knees with her kiss could handle brief shorts and a halter top with no trouble at all.

Joe cupped her face in his hands, kissing her lightly on her forehead. "Talk to me nice and I'll buy you an ice cream. It will go well with that pretty pink top and those sneakers."

"I'm not a child."

"No, but playing like one for a day won't hurt any of us."

"Stop watching them like a hawk. Joe is old enough to take care of himself. With his gift he's better able to tell the good from the bad than most."

Her attention on Josh, Pippa absently took a lick of her pistachio, chocolate, and peppermint ice cream cone. The four of them had taken refuge from the heat and the morning of shopping in a small park shaded by palms and large trees. Flowers abounded in beautifully tended beds. There were benches and tables. Children played in the background, watched by their mothers.

Josh eyed his dish of vanilla with disgust. He should have tried that Rocky Road stuff that Pippa had tried to convince him would appeal.

"She's flirting with him."

Pippa laughed. "She's doing a good job of it, too, if Joe's expression is anything to go by."

She studied the pair, liking the color blooming in Lyla's cheeks. Her friend looked better and more relaxed with each passing minute. Her laugh came more often, her smile quick and full. Joe looked younger, less imprisoned by that gravity that was as much a part of him as his dark eyes.

"Damn it, Pippa. My brother is vulnerable. In his personal life his gift is more a curse than a blessing."

He glared at her, his face tight. All morning he had watched the affinity growing between Lyla and Joe. Having finally made a real contact with his brother, he didn't want anything to strain the tie. Certainly not a ship board romance.

Pippa touched his hand, sliding her fingers through his clenched ones. "You can't protect him no matter how much you want to. Stop thinking with your brain and use your heart. Joe and Lyla are two fragile people. But it's a different kind of fragility. Where one is weak the other is strong."

Josh searched her face, a sudden thought deepening his anger. "Are you trying to set my brother up? Is that mind of yours so active that it constantly needs to be stirring up trouble, manipulating other people's lives?"

Pippa drew back, feeling the slap of his words as real blows. Her temperament could be volatile, anger one of her two least controlled emotions.

"You're a fool, Joshua Luck. A stupid, cold-blooded fool. I told you before, I don't manipulate. I offer. No one forced Joe to like Lyla. Nor she him. I just gave them a chance to meet. No more."

She rose, slammed her half-finished cone into the waste bin a half step away. "I'm leaving."

Josh got to his feet, realizing that he had hurt her in a way he hadn't anticipated. He reached for her, but she shrugged out of his hold.

"Damnit, Pippa, let me apologize."

She swung around, her hands on her hips. "Why should I?"

He stopped, caught by the logic of the unexpected question. He didn't have an answer, but even if he had, Pippa didn't give him a chance to use it.

"You may have the sexiest body I've ever seen, but your heart is a wasteland. I'm tired of being added up like a column of figures. I don't fit. I told you that in the beginning. Stop hurting me by trying to make me fit your image. I can't. More than that. I do not want to."

Tears glittered in her eyes. Furious at the weakness, she turned her head but not fast enough. Josh saw.

He groaned and pulled her into his arms, ignoring her struggles and the less-than-discreet names she was tossing at him. He tucked her head against his chest.

"You aren't supposed to cry."

"Will you shut up," she muttered into his shirt.

Suddenly the fight drained out of her. His body was strong, an unyielding bulwark between her and the world. Surely it would be all right to hang on for just a moment. Her arms crept around his waist. His chin came to rest on her hair.

"I'm not ever this soggy." she whispered.

His lips twisted at the description. "I never thought you were." He paused, needing to be honest but not accustomed to airing his feelings.

"I don't think either of us was prepared for this kind of emotion. I thought I was alone in feeling out of my depth. But you're not used to it either are you?"

"No," she admitted with a sigh. Lifting her head, she studied his face. Although his expression was smooth, she saw below the surface.

"I've had other relationships. Not many...five if you need the number. I don't handle closeness well at all. I tried. In my twenties I still believed I could do all the things other women did. I wanted a home and children, a man to share with. But I couldn't make the grade.

His needs got in the way of mine. My stories didn't work anymore. My concentration was shot. Nothing worked right. He was a good man, a caring person. He tried, I tried, and in the end we both knew trying wasn't enough.

I left. I gave him back his peace and took back my own. Four years later, I tried again. I was older, wiser, more secure, I told myself, and so was the man. This one lasted even less time. The man wasn't so willing to try, and I wasn't so willing to compromise. He left.

I was alone but really wiser. A year later my niece came to live with me. I found what I needed then. A family, but someone else's. I have two families now. I share their lives because they include me out of love. I give what I can and they don't ask for more.

If I find a man I care for, I share what I can. Soon there will be a great-niece or nephew and I will enjoy that but I will still have my freedom. Jason and Diana will be the parents and I will be the fairy godmother."

She smiled sadly but with a kind of defiance.

Josh cradled her face in his hands. "Is it enough, Pippa?"

"Ask yourself the same question. You don't intend to have children, and any marriage you have will be a bloodless union of minds. You tell me. Is it worth it? Where will your empire go? To Joe? He doesn't need it and I doubt he wants it. Oh, he will care for it out of love for you, but it isn't the same and you know it."

Neither moved. Both faced the future they had chosen.

"Are we wrong?"

She shook her head. "I'm not. I don't know about you. I can only guess."

"Hey, you two, break it up," Joe said, interrupting them. Lyla stood beside him, her glance carefully on Pippa's face. "Lunch is next on the schedule if I am to get back to the ship in time for my presentation."

Josh dropped his hands and stepped back. Pippa missed his warmth almost immediately.

"Brother, you have damnable timing. Remind me to return the favor," Josh said in exasperation.

Joe grinned. "You should pick a more private place for that kind of thing.'"

"I could say the same about you," Josh replied.

Lyla blushed. Joe took her hand, threading his fingers through hers. "Behave. Lyla isn't used to you."

Josh heard the subtle warning. Uneasy with the situation but learning not to jump, he tried a different approach. He attempted a smile in the younger woman's direction.

"By now, Pippa would have been glaring at me."

Lyla started. The almost friendly note in Josh's voice after the coolness of the morning was unexpected. She looked to Pippa for a clue to the change and found her retying her shoe.

"I'm not good at glaring," she murmured, feeling awkward. She had never been comfortable with repartee-type conversation.

"Get Pippa to teach you. It might come in handy sometime." Josh looked down at Pippa. "What are you doing?" he demanded, watching her struggle with her shoe for a moment.

What had started as a way to escape Joe's too perceptive gaze had become, in fact, a problem. "This stupid thing is knotted up somehow. It's about to cut off my circulation."

Josh bent down. "Let me see."

She moved her hands. He peered at it, finally rising to his full height. Reaching down, he caught her under her arms, lifting her, and setting her on the table.

"What are you doing?"

"Getting a better position. I refuse to squat down there to undo this mess. My bones aren't built for that position, not even when I was younger." He lifted her foot, almost toppling Pippa over in the process.

She scowled and he chuckled. "I'm new at this. Don't expect finesse."

"I don't expect anything, you great oaf," she said, laughing and glaring at the same time. He enjoyed tipping her over, the rat. "Just remember, retribution is sweet."

CHAPTER ELEVEN

"Come on, let's try a game of darts."

Pippa eyed the board on the pub wall. The restaurant that Joe had suggested was one of the island's best known. On the western perimeter of George Town, it offered a panoramic water view from its second-story elevation. Its specialty was seafood, from which it got its name. But as far as Pippa was concerned the best part was the English pub atmosphere, oaken booths, and English ale.

"Which one of us are you challenging?" Joe asked.

Pippa's head whipped around, her eyes alight with the joy of rediscovering a past time she had once enjoyed in her youth.

"Any of you."

"I don't think..." Joe began, only to close his mouth after a sharp jab from his brother's foot.

"Wouldn't you rather sit and enjoy a rest?" Josh murmured, watching her face with what he believed was a suitably hopeful expression.

"No, I would not," she stated flatly. "I'm not tired. You can't come on a trip like this and not try a little of everything." She finished the rest of her ale in one swallow.

"You want to try, Lyla?" Joe asked.

Lyla laughed. "Not me. I saw how good those men were. About the time I picked up a dart and stuck it in the ceiling, I'd clear the place. I don't think that would do too much for the management's idea of profit."

Pippa turned her head to eye the game. Disappointment wasn't her favorite feeling. She started when Joshua caught her hand and pulled her from the booth.

"Come on, woman. You look like a kid who just lost her favorite toy. I'll give you a game, but don't say I didn't warn you."

Pippa laughed delightedly. "I'm rusty, so it won't matter if you haven't played." In her excitement, she missed Joe's choke of amusement.

Lyla studied him as Josh and Pippa crossed the room. "What's that all about?"

"My brother is setting up our energetic leader. Josh has very few passions, but darts happens to be one of them. He'll beat her and anyone else in this room if he's really on."

Lyla frowned, glancing back to Pippa's glowing face. "That's not kind."

Joe caught her hand. "Not to you or me but watch. Pippa won't mind. She'll just find a way of evening the score."

"It's like they're in a duel of some kind." Lyla shook her head. "I couldn't be like that. I wouldn't want to fight."

"Nor I. But they aren't us. Josh has spent years with quietly dignified women who have about as much color as a cloud. Pippa is a palette of color, never the same twice. She splatters the human canvas with emotion."

Lyla looked at him, seeing his gift more clearly with every word. "That's beautiful," she murmured, watching his eyes.

He shrugged, not accustomed to immediate acceptance. Lyla seemed to like his perception and believing that could be dangerous for him. When he trusted, he gave more and that was a double-edged sword for one such as he.

People seldom wanted someone to know them so intimately. History had taught mankind the value of secrecy, of guarding one's thoughts and emotions.

"Let's not spoil the day analyzing each other."

"Why do you do that?" Lyla asked.

"What?"

"Draw back. If I thought being psychic was a contagious disease, I wouldn't be sitting here. I don't mind that you have an ability to see deeper."

She looked down at their linked hands. "In fact, I like it. It makes me feel safe again. You really know I didn't do all those horrible things. I'm not the woman that the media made me out to be."

Joe studied her down bent head, suddenly feeling pain, a different kind of hurt for a different kind of woman. He could have damned himself for a fool for not having foreseen this possibility.

Because he was so accustomed to women either being attracted to his gift or repelled by it, he had let himself be blinded by Lyla's matter-of-fact acceptance. It hadn't occurred to him that she might have a deeper reason for allowing him close.

"I'm not always right," he said roughly, wanting to disillusion her.

Lyla lifted her chin, her eyes locking with his. "Are you trying to warn me?" she murmured, confused by his tone and the words. "No one is a hundred per cent anything.

"Don't make me into a superman. I'm not. I can bleed, too."

Too intimately acquainted with pain not to recognize it in others, Lyla hesitated. Although it was the last thing she wanted, somehow, she had hurt Joe. Her fingers tightened on his.

"What did I say or do wrong?"

Unable to look away from her troubled face, Joe searched for the words to explain. There were none. For he had been the one to blunder, not Lyla. He had permitted someone to come too close before looking for the reality of truth. Now he had the price to pay.

"You've done nothing wrong." He managed a smile and a direct look that cloaked the turmoil of his thoughts.

Lyla studied him for a moment longer, sensing but not understanding the sudden distance between them. It was as if she had lost something special, something she barely understood yet.

Wanting that closeness back, she reached out to him. She felt the tension in his hand. Hurt, she released him, lingering for one instant before the final break of contact.

A burst of laughter from the vigorous dart game in the background seemed an insult. Weariness settled on her shoulders. All she wanted was the privacy of her cabin.

"Can we go back to the ship?"

Joe's brows rose at the question. He didn't like the hurt he could clearly see on her face. He hadn't meant to push her away, hadn't known she would feel his retreat.

"We haven't ordered our lunch," he reminded her. "We have to leave as soon as we eat anyway."

Lyla glanced over her shoulder to the dart game in progress. She needed to concentrate on something, anything besides the man across from her.

Despite being dwarfed by an assortment of masculine shapes, Pippa's slim figure stood out in the crowd. She was laughing, teasing Josh and those in the crowd that had gathered to watch the competition.

She smiled at the way the older woman radiated such confidence, such enthusiasm. She seemed to light up the room.

"Looks like Josh might have met his match," she murmured, more to herself than to Joe.

"The game isn't over yet," Joe drawled.

The tone of his voice, the edge of assurance she had never heard before got her attention. Lyla looked back at him, glaring.

"You sound like you want Pippa to lose."

Joe shrugged, not really interested in the game or the outcome. He already knew the answer to both.

Lyla studied him for a long moment. "You're different. I don't know what I said and you won't tell me."

"You did nothing. I don't lie."

" I don't believe you."

"Impasse."

Lyla started to rise, but Joe caught her hand. "I thought you trusted me?"

She looked into his eyes. seeing past the barriers to the hurt beneath. "Tell me, Joe. Whatever it is, tell me."

He felt the beat of her pulse, the urgency of the rate, the demand of the words, the fear in her look. He could all but taste her confusion. He didn't want to answer yet he couldn't continue to hurt her with his silence no matter what the cost.

"All my life people have gotten close to me or thrown me out because of what I can do. I was fool enough to think you weren't one of those. You seemed so unaffected by my power." He grimaced at the last word.

"I told you it didn't matter to me."

"But it does. You said that, too."

Mentally, she did a swift check of what she had said to him. She found no answers there.

"How?"

131

"You said I could tell you hadn't done all of those things you were accused of."

"Can't you?"

He inclined his head slowly. "Yes."

Lyla struggled through the maze of words for the truth. Suddenly, like a harsh light after complete darkness, she understood. In the understanding, she realized that maybe he was right. Joe could give her what no one else she knew on earth could.

Complete belief in her innocence because he knew she hadn't done anything wrong. Without realizing it, she had let his psychic ability give her the security and strength she needed.

Joe saw her change of expression. His own reflected his burden. "Do you see now?"

Lyla didn't know what to do. She hadn't been conscious of her response to him on that level. Everything had seemed so natural, so easy after the last four years of pain, lies and struggle just to survive one more day. Empty words seemed so banal, but they were all she had.

"I'm sorry. Truly, I didn't consciously think of what I was feeling with you. It just was..." She spread her hands, defeated by the words she couldn't find to explain more fully.

"Don't be for the truth."

"I didn't mean to hurt you. You've been so kind."

He gave a short bark of unamused laughter.

"Kind. That's me. The gentle fortune teller with all the answers."

For one moment he allowed his past to emerge in all its bitter glory. Then as quickly as he released the lava flow of emotion, he shut it off, his expression clearing.

"Don't worry about it. I do like you and I do know you didn't do those things. I am glad you came out with us. You deserve to find happiness again. I like being a part of opening that door for you." He smiled. Every word was the truth.

Lyla knew she had never seen a more terrible look in a man's eyes than in Joe's. As far as her mind and eye could see, lay only emotional barrenness. She wanted to cry. But because he waited, because something told her that she had to give him this moment of agreement, she managed to smooth her expression.

She touched his hand, quickly, for to linger was to invite more of the need that was growing by the moment. He didn't want her comfort. He only wanted distance and safety, two desires she knew very well.

"I'm glad you and Pippa were there."

His hand clenched, once reflexively, then he pulled it across the table to disappear beneath the surface. Touching her was a mistake until he had more control over his emotions and his gift.

It would be too easy to look past this moment to the future. Although that knowledge might give him peace, it would also mean that he was stepping over a line he had drawn years ago.

He never used his gift for his own benefit.

"Look." He nodded to the game that was drawing to a close. "It appears Pippa is finding out just how good Josh is."

Lyla glanced over her shoulder, glad for the slight dimness of the room. Tears that she could not allow to fall blurred her vision, but she answered as though she could see clearly.

"You were right. She doesn't look upset at all." The sound of Pippa's laughter rang out, bright, young, and free. Lyla wished suddenly that she had one half the older woman's zest for life. Pippa would have known how to touch Joe without hurting him.

CHAPTER TWELVE

Pippa studied Josh's form, torn between irritation at the trick he had played on her and a sportsman's admiration for his style. His movements were deliberately graceful, smooth, and perfectly timed. Again and again his dart had pierced the center of the target. His accuracy had grown with each shot.

She had played well herself but nothing she had done had come close to his expertise. Without realizing it, she smiled as his last shot sailed home.

"I think I hate you," she announced, laughing.

He turned, his eyes alight with his win and the challenge of putting one over on his bright-eyed temptress.

"You deserved to get beat," he replied, grinning. "Arrogance is not an attractive attribute."

"Look who's talking. I don't see any modesty from where I'm standing."

He came to her side, slipped an arm around her waist, and drew her close. "Keep that pouty expression on your face for one more minute and I promise you I will kiss it off," he murmured below the noise of the crowd.

Pippa glanced around, liking this teasing male very much. She had hoped he would loosen up, but even she hadn't expected the kind of devilment of which Josh seemed capable.

"I could call your bluff."

"Go ahead. I dare you."

She almost did it. It would have been so easy to lift her lips that fraction of an inch. But they did have an audience, and when Josh touched her, she might forget that little detail.

Passion would blot out everything but a need to join her body to his. Restraint was no longer possible and they both knew it. The next time they came together the fire would burn them both.

"You rat," she whispered.

He laughed down at her, feeling stronger and younger than he ever had. Pippa made him believe in desire and wanting and being alive. Control was a device to heighten his pleasure. Inhibitions added spice and winning fanned the need for more. He hugged her once then let her go.

"Tonight," he said roughly as he set her free.

"Tonight. Tomorrow and as long as the sea stretches beneath us," she returned. "Thirteen days of Luck."

"Thirteen nights of Stars."

She wrinkled her nose and made a face a mischievous urchin would have approved.

He grinned. "I thought it was good."

"It was terrible," she disagreed as they started back to their booth.

"No worse than yours. I thought writers had more imagination."

"I thought I was very imaginative."

"Are you two still at it?" Joe asked as they sat down. Before either could answer, he added, "Don't get too comfortable. The waitress just came over to say our table in the dining room is ready."

"Good, I'm starved," Pippa said. "I love lobster and most seafood."

Josh rose and threaded his fingers through Pippa's. "I'm beginning to think you love almost anything."

She gave him a flirty look, batting her lashes for good measure. "I'll never tell."

Lyla watched the exchange, wishing she could share the same kind of fun with Joe. But his face was closed to her now, his hands tucked in his pockets. As body language went, his was saying NO TOUCHING in capital letters.

She was alone in a crowd of four. The isolation was surprisingly complete. Lunch was more of the same. Pippa and Josh created an atmosphere that was alive with innuendo and challenge. Joe and she took part, but the other couple didn't seem aware that their participation was token at best. When they finally returned to the ship, Lyla was well on the way to a headache.

"Ms. Carson?"

Lyla stopped as the purser approached. "Yes?"

"There's a man looking for you. His name is Edward Donovan. He said that you would know him and that he would be waiting for you in the lounge on the promenade deck."

Paling at the mention of the DEA agent who had first interrogated her, Lyla inclined her head. "Thank you," she said faintly, not meaning a word of the common courtesy. The last person she ever wanted to see again was Agent Donovan.

The purser looked at her curiously before walking away. Pippa touched Lyla's arm, her expression reflecting her concern.

"What is it? Who is this Donovan creature?"

She had vague memory of the name as belonging to one of law enforcement people involved in Lyla's case.

Lyla tried a shrug with muscles too tense to carry off the gesture. "He's the man who initiated the sting operation that I ended up taking the blame for in the beginning."

"I thought you said the trial was over."

"It is. My boss was found guilty. But there are such things as appeals. He did have the money to hire the best legal minds in the country."

Lyla stared down the corridor. "I'll have to see what Donovan wants." The thought made her shiver with reaction. For a few precious moments today, she had forgotten the past.

Joe watched Lyla, feeling the waves of fear and pain as tangible scrapes across the fabric of his mind. He wanted to hold her, tell her that nothing or no one would hurt her again. But he knew that was a futile wish, for the future was alive with darkness. He could feel the clouds gathering around them, all of them. He glanced at his brother to find Josh studying him.

"It's bad, isn't it?" Josh said quietly, speaking below the conversation going on between the two women.

"Damn bad," Joe agreed flatly.

As little as a week ago, Josh would have questioned Joe's certainty. Today he accepted his knowledge as though it were tangible fact.

"Any details or just a blanket warning?"

Joe shook his head, wishing he was someplace private. There was so much sensory input that sorting through the maze was nearly impossible with his mind being assailed by the emotions of those around him.

"The last at the moment," he admitted.

Pippa turned, catching both men's eyes. "I don't think she ought to meet this person alone. She's not listening to me."

Josh studied the younger woman, seeing the pride he had missed earlier. "She's right. If you had a family with you, you would want them."

"None of you are family and you don't want to get mixed up in this mess. It's dirty and no one really seems to care who gets a mud bath. The guilty or the innocent, it's all the same to them."

Pippa's eyes flashed fire at the despair in Lyla's voice. "That settles it. I'm going. A lounge is a public place. That creep can't stop me being there." Her look dared anyone to object.

Josh dropped an arm over her shoulders, hugging her to his side. "Down, my silver-haired dragon. I'm coming too."

"So am I. I have time," Joe added, moving to Lyla's side. He took her hand, resisting her efforts to pull it free.

Lyla stared at the small ring of support she had suddenly acquired. Tears welled in her eyes.

"You can't," she whispered, gazing at each in turn. "You've been very kind, but this is my problem."

"We're making it ours." Again, it was Josh who took the lead. "As far as I can see, you've got precious little power to bargain for anything. Between us, we do. Plus none of us is good at losing. Whether you want us or not, you have us."

Pippa nodded vigorously, her expression vivid with the challenge. "He's right. Listen to him. We've got clout and the time. Let us be there with you."

Lyla glanced at Joe. She could have refused the older couple's support, but the insistent look in Joe's eyes was another story entirely.

"You're sure?" she asked him, searching his face.

"I'm positive."

He could have added that if she didn't accept their help, her future would not resolve well. He could have said that all of their futures hinged on this 'mess', as she called it. He didn't know the details yet, but he understood how important her agreement was.

"All right."

Lyla squeezed his hand. She had been alone for so long she hadn't thought to ever have someone to believe in her again. Now she had three believers. Her shaky smile encompassed them all.

"Thank you."

Josh took her arm and turned her toward the aft of the ship. "We haven't done anything yet."

They made a solid wall two deep as they moved down the deck. Because they had returned too late for lunch on the ship and too early for dinner, the aisle was almost empty of other traffic. They entered the lounge together, a united front for the skirmish ahead.

One man sat at the rear of the lounge, watching the door. He studied the four of them as they moved to join him. His brows rose as Lyla sat down first, then the others.

"I don't think an audience is necessary."

"We do." Both Josh and Joe spoke together.

Josh glanced at his brother's set face and leaned back in his chair. He'd play the second string for now. When Pippa's hand slipped into his, he glanced at her. Her look applauded his course.

A warm feeling that had nothing to do with the situation filled him. No one, in all his life, had ever shown him that kind of approval. He hadn't even known he needed it. His hand tightened on hers before he turned back to the man who, at the moment, was dealing the cards.

Donovan frowned. Absently rotating the glass he held, he studied the three he hadn't expected. "I don't think this is wise. I hardly think your board of directors will be pleased with your interest in a drug investigation, Mr. Luck," he pointed out, speaking to Joshua first.

When Joshua didn't respond, he turned his attention to the younger, possibly softer version of the elder Luck. The last thing this situation needed was more publicity. There had been too damn much of it already.

"Or your involvement, Mr. Luck. It won't do your psychic reputation much good either. Most people don't even believe in this fortune-telling stuff."

Joe smiled grimly, he could feel the man's frustration and determination. "Are you always in the habit of investigating innocent citizens? Interesting technique. Hardly the kind of thing guaranteed to endear you to ordinary people if it were to get out, into the media perhaps."

"Are you threatening me?"

"I could return the question."

The two men stared at each other, neither prepared to back down. Josh tipped the scales.

"You might want to tread very carefully, Donovan. Men in my position know a hell of a lot that should be kept under wraps. Rattle me or those I care about, and I hit back. Hard!"

Donovan's head swiveled between the Lucks. "You don't know what you're involved in and who this woman is."

"We know." Pippa spoke for the first time, leaning forward in her chair.

Donovan's frown deepened to a scowl which he turned on Lyla. She faced him, something she had been unable to do in the past. Feeling guilty and dirtied by the investigation, she had let this man bully her as he was trying to do to her friends. For the first time, she looked beyond her fear and defeat to the truth.

"I told them everything," she stated flatly. "I had nothing to hide and I am tired of acting as though I do."

"That was a mistake, Lyla," he said, his voice laced with innuendo.

Lyla paled but held her ground. This time she had people who took her word. She wouldn't betray them by running or caving in to opposition.

"I don't think so."

"Why don't you get to the point? Lyla is on vacation, and we have things to do. Say what you came here to say and then let us alone," Josh commanded.

"I didn't come to say anything. I came to get Lyla."

Lyla stiffened, fear slicing through the fragile composure she had managed to build. Josh and Joe straightened, each wearing almost the same set expression. Neither looked prepared to hand Lyla over.

"You have a warrant?"

"I don't need one. I'm not arresting her. It's for her own good. An appeal for a new trial is in the works. She's our main witness. We want her somewhere safe until this thing is settled."

"Like hell," Joe exploded in uncharacteristic anger. "Appeals take time. What are you planning to do, keep her locked up indefinitely? When will she be able to get on with her life? Or has this country suddenly decided to renege on the promises it made in the Constitution?"

"Watch it, Luck. This is DEA business and none of yours. In case you've been too lost in the world of make-believe, we're in a war here. We use whatever weapons we have to make what little difference we can."

Without realizing it, the bitterness of a good man trying to do an impossible job crept into his words.

"I don't give a damn what I have to do. Navaro is going to prison and if that means playing nursemaid to one Lyla Carson, then I'm going to sit on her toes until hell freezes over."

He laid his palms flat on the table and glared at them all in turn. "And no one better get in my way."

Joe leaned forward in his chair. "And I'll tell you that you and your damn investigation have done enough damage."

"If your little girlfriend hadn't been so naive, she wouldn't be in this fix now. She made her choices. It's too late to scream they're giving her indigestion."

"I'm not going with you."

Donovan's eyes locked with Lyla's. "You are. You have no choice."

"She has a choice," Pippa inserted. "We're giving her one. As for her being safe, a determined assassin will have his way no matter what the precautions. She's no safer with you than she would be with us. Dead is dead."

Lyla surprised them all with a choke of amusement. "Thanks a lot."

Pippa shrugged, her blouse falling off one shoulder. Donovan glowered. Josh pulled the fabric back into place and Joe rose.

"This is getting us nowhere. The truth is that, as far as I can see, you can't do anything. You can't arrest Lyla, and kidnapping is a federal offense. And anything else is going to get you some publicity neither you nor your department is going to want."

"You're bluffing."

"Call it then."

His movements jerky with restrained fury, Donovan pushed to his feet. "You'll think differently if one or all of you end up in the hospital. If you're lucky, it won't be the morgue. These guys play for keeps.

Drugs are megabucks. Anything can be had at a price. At least with us, she has a fighting chance. You've just given her nothing."

He took a business card from his pocket, scribbled a number on the back, and tossed it on the table in front of Lyla.

"When it gets too hot out here for you, give us a call. We might still be interested in keeping you alive."

"What a thoroughly unpleasant man," Pippa murmured, watching Donovan stride out of the lounge. "No wonder you had such a hard time."

Lyla picked up the card, looking at it without really seeing it. "I don't like him, but it is because of him that Navaro came to trial. Donovan wouldn't believe I was sophisticated enough to pull off the kind of operation that Navaro had.

In spite of his superiors, Donovan kept digging when everyone else was ready to convict me. He drove me crazy with questions and frightened me into remembering things I hadn't even realized I knew."

She glanced up, smiling shakily. "He's tough and he has no respect for my intelligence and no time for any courtesy, but he treated me better than anyone else did then."

"That still doesn't give him the right to try to force you to live like a criminal for an indefinite period," Pippa argued.

"But the alternative is to involve you. He was right about that. Navaro's organization is nothing to mess around with. He's got money in places that the DEA couldn't get to."

Lyla suppressed a shiver, determined to be honest. All their lives depended on it. "What I know is at least half the case against Navaro. Kill me and he just might walk."

For a moment, no one spoke. Josh looked at Pippa, trying to imagine how he would feel if she was the one who paid the penalty for their interference. The twist in his gut told him that he would care too much.

And Joe? He glanced at his brother. They were just establishing a tie. He would truly be alone if Joe was the cost. Then he looked at Lyla. Pippa had been right all along. Lyla had been caught in a situation that she couldn't have foreseen. She deserved more than fear and a price on her head as a future.

Joe stared at no one. Rather, his thoughts turned inward to the source of peace and knowledge that had sustained him through every crisis in his life. For as long as he could remember, he had been helping people to the limits of his strength and power.

Although the stakes were higher this time and potentially more costly, he had only one choice. For better or worse he was in.

Pippa divided her gaze between the other three. She didn't need to make a decision. Hers had been made the moment Lyla had up ended her purse. That very first meeting had touched her deeply. She had never been able to turn away from damaged creatures. Prices one paid in life for choices had never mattered to her. The only goal was to live as well and as deeply as possible.

"I think we've all decided," she said quietly when no one seemed disposed to speak. "I'm staying."

"So am I," Josh seconded.

"And me," Joe added firmly.

Lyla shook her head. "I shouldn't let you."

Joe took her hand, looking into her dark eyes. "But you will."

She hesitated, wishing she was brave enough to turn them down. Then slowly, praying that she wasn't going to damage one or all of them irreparably, she nodded.

"Now we need a plan," Pippa announced, propping her elbows on the table. "If Donovan found you, then it's a cinch this creep Navaro can, too. Since this ship is already filled with strangers, we don't stand a snowball's chance at finding out if there is already someone on board."

"I don't think we have to worry about that. It's the newcomers we've got to watch. Remember, no one knew Lyla was booked on this cruise. There wouldn't have been time to plant someone," Josh reasoned.

"No, but there has been time to buy someone," Joe pointed out.

Lyla made a face. "Thanks. I needed that."

Joe tucked her against his side. "Lying to ourselves is suicide."

"At least we have Joe's infrared mind. He's our ace, our early warning."

Lyla glanced at Josh, surprised at the description. "What do you mean?"

"If I understand what Joe has been telling me, strong emotion, like an intent to kill someone, is a red flag, highly visible and very traceable to someone with his sensitivity."

"You're thinking what I'm thinking," Joe commented.

Josh grinned, looking decidedly dangerous. "Until this mess is over or we can think of a better way, you two are joined at the hip."

"But we can't. You have your commitments," Lyla objected.

"That doesn't preclude my having a private life," Joe replied, watching her intently.

She frowned. "I don't like this."

Pippa touched Lyla's free hand. "Listen to them. Joe is your best chance until we can figure out something better."

Lyla sighed. Arguing with these three was impossible. "I'm just glad you all are here. I don't even want to think what would have happened otherwise."

Pippa rose with Josh right behind her. "I, for one, could use a rest. I know you have to work first, Joe. I wish there had been room left for me and Josh to attend your presentation. Since we can't, we'll retire to our cabins and then meet again for dinner. How about that chef's restaurant on the island you were telling us about?" Pippa suggested.

"Good idea. Lyla being alone is not a possibility. So, she can come either to my presentation or she can stick with you two. It will have to be backstage if you come with me," he warned.

"With you. I don't mind where I sit. I would like to see what you do."

He could hear the sincerity in her voice. A part of him relaxed at the knowledge she really did want to understand this part of him. He nodded and urged Lyla to her feet.

"We need to hurry. I am cutting it close as it is."

Josh watched his brother and Lyla for a moment. The two looked like a unit as they walked away. Time and timing didn't seem to be an issue for either of them.

"I don't know what you've gotten all of us into, Pippa Weldon, but I'm not sorry I came on this cruise," Josh said quietly.

She angled to face him. Searching his expression for the truth, she saw only a reinforcement to his words.

"Thanks for throwing your weight into this. I would have understood if you had wanted out, considering the way you seem to feel about Lyla."

"I was wrong about her. She's what you said, not what I thought."

Pippa touched his face, her fingers lingering over the strong bone of his jaw. "I really like you, Joshua Luck." His smile was a rainbow of emotion. She bathed in it and returned it to the giver.

"I wonder if it is as much as I like you." He tucked her hand in the crook of his arm. "Shall we go find out?"

"I thought you would never ask."

CHAPTER THIRTEEN

Josh shut the door on Pippa's suite. She turned in his arms, smiling. "I'm glad I'm not twenty any longer."

His brows raised at the comment. "Apropos to what?"

"This." She fit her curves to his, letting him feel the length of her body.

Even though he was taller than she was, they fit as though they were parts of one body. His muscles rippled as she slid her hands up his back. She tipped back her head to find him watching her with an intensity that lit a fire in her blood. As if she needed more heat!

He cradled her face in his palms, looking into her eyes as though he could see past tomorrow. He had never met a woman like Pippa. None had ever made him forget everything but having her in his arms, claiming her as his.

"You are some kind of woman, Pippa Weldon. I don't think I've ever known anyone who could be so honest."

"Does it bother you?" She searched his expression.

He shook his head, grinning. "No. It makes me feel all things male, primitive, territorial, dangerous. Definitely not pleasant or relaxing..."

Laughing, she stretched up to kiss his lips. "I'm very glad that woman was that stupid about you. I don't think I would have met you otherwise."

His hands slipped to her shoulders, pulling her closer yet. He didn't want to remember the life he had left behind. He knew, no matter what the next thirteen days brought, he would never be the same again.

"I'm glad Lisa felt like that, too," he admitted, meaning it for the first time. He had needed the hammer blow of her description to get his attention, to make him see what he had become.

"Pretty name."

He nodded. He would not lie to this woman in his arms, not with silence or words. "She is an attractive woman. Some would call her beautiful."

"Should I be jealous?" she asked huskily.

His hands moved lower, cupping her breasts in his palms. The fabric of her halter didn't hide her immediate response to his touch.

"Don't ask stupid questions."

She giggled deep in her throat. She could feel the fire of wanting build. Sliding her fingers under the edge of his shirt, she found the thick pelt of hair on his chest. The strands were silky, warm from his body heat. He jerked at her first touch, then leaned into the intimate caress.

"You like that."

"You didn't do it because you thought I wouldn't."

She smiled as her fingers found his nipples. Teasing them, she watched his face grow taut with desire. When he returned the favor, she inhaled deeply, drinking in his scent as one starving for the fragrance.

"What do you like?"

"Anything you are prepared to give," he breathed roughly as he released the tie at the back of her neck. The fabric slid away from her curves.

Pippa leaned into his hands, the heat of his body driving out the need for words. His touch was gentle yet there was strength implicit in his caresses, strength to hold, strength to challenge. Her lashes drifted down, muting the light in the cabin, focusing her thoughts and senses only on the man.

"Beautiful doesn't begin to describe you," he whispered as her top fell to her waist, checking at the band of her slacks. "Why are we standing here when we could be over there?"

"I couldn't wait."

He laughed huskily. Her candor was another spur to his need. "Damn you, woman, is there any guile in you?"

"No." She pulled his head down to hers. "There are too many words in you. Action now, talk later." Her mouth covered his, taking and giving with equal fervor.

Josh lifted her in his arms, the romantic gesture as foreign to his nature as the passion blazing to life in his body. He carried her to the bed, dropping on one knee on the spread. Her hands held him so that when he would have released her, he found separation impossible.

"I meant to go slow."

"Next time."

Pippa raise her hands, pushing the shirt up to his shoulders. His muscles moved sleekly beneath the bronzed flesh. His maturity had given him more than age.

There was a presence, again that regality that she found impossible to ignore. It called to her, a silent voice of magic she had never heard before. Her hands smoothed over the angles and planes of his body.

His groans were pleas and commands for more. Never had undressing a man been such a pleasure. She hardly noticed that her own clothes now lay on the floor in a tangled heap with his. Sunlight poured through the porthole, highlighting them both.

A Rodin sculpture could not have been more superbly wrought. The poses were classic, more than passion, than simple wanting. Emotion shone on their faces, more perhaps than either realized.

Pippa was the falcon who had always soared on the passion of the moment and Josh was the eagle who had never known the ecstasy of flight. Strong creatures, beings forged through time, circumstances, and pain, they came together as equals.

Josh rose over her, looking into Pippa's pale eyes as she arched up to meet his thrust to join them as one. Her name was on his lips as her warmth closed around him.

His was a whisper as Pippa pulled him down into her arms.

"I hoped it would be like this," Pippa whispered, the fullness of their mating so new she had to pause to savor the sensation.

"You sound surprised," he murmured.

Josh gently teased her breast, his tongue wrapping around her nipple. The shivers of delight racing over Pippa's skin were tiny quivers to titillate his senses.

Her fingers tangled in his hair, lifting his head so that their eyes met. "I am. I had not thought this kind of completeness was possible." Her faint smile held both sadness and a touch of triumph.

He stroked her length, enjoying the feel of her in his hands. "Neither had I. Strange we had to wait so long to find it."

And each other, Pippa could have added but didn't. For one moment, she fought the urge to move outside the rules they had set.

The madness of need that made this union more than either of them was prepared for was the most exquisite kind of torture. She closed her eyes to shut out his image and found instead an even stronger one in her mind. Fantasy, reality.

As his hands began to move over her, she didn't know where one began and the other ended. Whatever control she had slipped from her. His body belonged to hers. His mind held no thoughts beyond her. She opened her eyes, looking into his as passion lifted them higher. His groans matched hers. His heat tapped her own as the fire raged out of control.

Her nails dug into his back. Just on the brink of her consciousness hovered the goal they were straining to reach. She could not lose touch now. It was imperative that they be together.

"Hold me," he commanded, driving forward.

Pippa responded, rushing to meet him in a wild surge that took him by surprise.

Nova. A blazing inferno of instantaneous light and heat. Then the little death, a slow slide back to reality. The comfort and closeness of arms around satiated bodies. A whisper, a gentleness of passion shared and spent to the last drop. Silence.

Pippa opened her eyes, staring at the face on the pillow next to hers. Sweat added a sheen of richness to his skin. She reached out, stroking his face, her fingers sliding through the damp hair at his temples.

"Did I tell you how sexy you are?" she asked softly.

Josh looked at her, smiling at the question and the woman assured enough to be vulnerable.

"No, but I would love listening to why."

She kissed his lips, her tongue tracing the outline. Josh rolled on his back and pulled her onto his chest.

"If you keep that up. We'll be back to not talking again."

"Tease."

His hands cradled her breasts, lifting the mounds, gently pushing them together.

"How can someone so slender be built so perfectly?" he murmured whimsically.

"Genes."

Pippa settled over his hips, wiggling a little to find just the right spot to tantalize them both.

Josh nudged her, grinning at the quick stirring of her body. Her nipples flowered eagerly. He rewarded each with a stroke of his tongue and a kiss.

"We should be resting," Pippa reminded him, her eyes alight with wicked intent.

"I've never felt less like resting in my life," Josh returned bluntly, laughing when she blushed. "I would like to know how you managed that?"

She batted her eyes at him. "Practice. Don't you think I did it well?"

"Superbly." He pulled her down so that her lips hovered an inch from his. "As you do everything."

"Compliments. I love them."

"Then be prepared to drown in them. I think I have a million waiting just for you."

"Flatterer."

He kissed her deeply, and when he raised his head, they were both breathing hard. "You'll earn them. As will I." With that the joining was made.

Lyla moved away from Joe as he closed the door to her cabin. She thought of what she had learned about the man she was coming to like too much for her peace of mind.

She had seen him stand in front of an audience, explaining about his gift and then offering a demonstration of how he worked. She, like the people in the crowd, had been amazed at what he could know with just a touch.

She had felt moments of attraction throughout the day, tiny flickers of interest that she hadn't felt in years. She had thought she had seen the same kind of awareness in him. A quick glance, a certain look in his eyes. He had made her laugh, relax, enjoy the day with him.

They had come to collect her things. "I don't think this is a good idea," Lyla muttered unhappily. She watched Joe check her cabin. Being cooped up with him on a daily, probably hourly basis was beginning to assume epic proportions.

Her feelings, new though they were, made being comfortable in his company almost impossible. Had she any privacy perhaps she could have found a measure of control. Instead, she had to find her balance with him watching, maybe even feeling her emotions.

Joe turned to study her. The animation and color had left her face. The new colorful outfit she wore seemed almost garish against her pale, nervous expression.

"Then what do you suggest?" he demanded suddenly, angry at the way she was apparently prepared to roll over and play dead because the going got tough. "I leave you here at the mercy of heaven-only-knows-who? Or maybe all of us should just pretend that we don't know you?"

"It's not your problem." Even to herself, she sounded repetitious.

"You're beginning to sound like a broken record. I know the past hasn't been the best place to learn about trust, but this is now. We aren't going anywhere, and we want to help."

"Why?" ·

"Why not?"

Joe came to her and lifted her out of the chair. Just when he thought she was making progress, the past came back to bury her in that terrible helplessness. Anger grew, at her, at the situation, and his own inability to do more.

"Damn you, woman, fight for yourself. Help us to help you. Or are you so weak that you surrender at the first sign of trouble?"

Lyla stared into his fiery eyes, stunned at the temper she had unleashed. Because to tell him the whole was to burden him with what he had already refused, she settled for a half truth.

"I'm tired, Joe. I'm tired of fighting battles I'm not sure I can win. I'm tired of the whispers and dirty looks. I'm tired of looking over my shoulder.

I'm tired of being alone. But more than all of those, I can't trust myself or anyone else anymore. Do you and Josh and Pippa have any idea what you're asking of me? You're all strangers, chancemet people I barely know. Your own brother half believes I did it."

"Did he say so?"

"His attitude did."

"Josh wouldn't bother with hiding behind any kind of attitude and he damn sure wouldn't let himself be entangled in anyone's affairs unless he had a good reason."

"How about Pippa as a reason? Neither of us could have missed the fire that is between them. He wants her, and for whatever reason, she wants to help me."

Joe shook his head before she even finished speaking. "You're wrong. Josh doesn't work that way, and even if he did, I think Pippa would see through that kind of maneuver."

His gaze held hers as he added, "But all of that is an excuse. The real reason you don't want us is because you're afraid we'll leave you as the rest of the people around you have done. You think you don't know any of us enough to trust us."

Lyla closed her eyes, gathering her strength. He was putting into words every emotion that she was feeling, the confusion, the fear.

"Yes," she said quietly. "My own family left when I needed them most and it almost finished me. I can't let myself depend on anyone again. I may not survive the next time."

Joe stared at her closed face, understanding the depth of her disillusionment. He shook her once, gently, demanding her attention. He waited until she looked at him.

"None of us will bailout on you. That is a promise. But even if that was not true, you simply have no other choice unless you either lay your head on a block and wait for the ax or deposit yourself into Donovan's questionable care. Right now, we're your only chance."

Lyla saw the strength in his face, heard the certainty in his voice. Both were resources she needed desperately. Hope, a forgotten dream, flickered. Trust. Such a small word to demand so much.

"It's your choice, Lyla. You have to make it," Joe said, his voice softening. His hands on her arms gentled, stroking rather than holding. He felt the tension leave her body. A long sigh and she slowly dropped her head to his chest like a spent child.

"I want to believe in all of you," she admitted huskily. His scent wrapped around her like a warm blanket on a rainy night. "I want to believe in me, too."

Joe pulled her close, fighting the urge to pick her up and carry her away where no one would ever bother her again.

"You will. It will take time, but you will believe again if you want it badly enough." He rested his chin on her hair.

Lyla wrapped her arms around his waist and savored the silence and comfort of the moment. It had been forever since anyone had held her. She hadn't known how much she needed this kind of undemanding contact.

As the silence between them lengthened, the one element she had sought to control slipped its tether. Her senses sharpened, sound, feel and sight suddenly hypersensitive. She raised her head.

He looked into her eyes and read the awakening desire.

"Don't do this to yourself or to me," he said roughly, fighting the battle for both of them. "You're vulnerable and, damn it, so am I."

She could no more have stopped the words than her last breath. "I want you."

Joe felt his barriers shake. He fought the urge to throw away his beliefs, his experiences and just take tomorrow in his hands.

"You want someone. You've been alone and fighting a losing war. You're letting that cloud your thinking. I won't be used like that."

He put her from him, frowning deeply. Raking his fingers through his hair, he increased the distance between them. To touch her was to lose the battle within himself.

Lyla watched him, frozen by his rejection, stunned by the depth of her need. Could he be right? She had so little experience. Her whole life had been a struggle to achieve, to finish college, to start a career, to make a home for herself. She'd had little time for a deep relationship, only a short term encounters that had suffered from the demands of her professional choices.

"I didn't mean to touch you," she protested, taking a step toward him.

He held her off with an abrupt gesture. "You aren't the only one carrying scars. I won't put a price on my help but don't expect me to give you more than I can. Laying myself open to the kind of hurt this situation could involve is not on the books. I'm more of a survivor than that."

They faced each other, both trying to understand, to find a way out of the past to the promise of the future and the reality of the present.

"I am not so dead to everything not to know when a man sees me as an attractive woman."

She faced him squarely, daring him to deny those few seconds of connection. The quick look then the turn away of denial. Hers and his.

"You wanted me earlier."

He wanted to deny what she was saying. She deserved better than lies and he was a man who only dealt in truth.

"Yes, I feel something. But I also know that this situation is a minefield of emotional danger for all of us. I am no masochist. Nor am I the kind of man to take advantage."

His brows rose and she felt the first stirring of a very real anger and insult. "You think I am so weak that I would be or am that easy?"

"Not weak nor easy." He sighed deeply. "Emotions are tricky and often deceptive."

"I thought your gift gave you clearer sight than that."

Joe shook his head. His expression was a study in sadness he would never have betrayed if he hadn't been reacting rather than thinking.

"I am not infallible, and there are a number of blind areas to my power. Don't make me into a god. I don't measure up. I'm only a man."

"I never thought you were a god."

She spread her hands, wishing she had the words to reach him. Because she had learned few of the tricks that many women seemed to know from birth, she opted for honesty.

"I can't pretend not to be affected by you. I don't have that kind of sophistication. Even if I did, I'm just too tired to try." Sighing wearily, she turned from him.

Joe watched her back for a moment before he, too, sighed. "This isn't getting us anywhere. Why don't we just relax, take each hour as it comes and be friends?"

Lyla stared at the sky framed by the port opening. Clear blue and bright, it was a circle of freedom that might never really be hers.

Friends? Could they manage so easy a relationship? Her emotions weren't calm, weren't friendly. Yet did she have any other choice but to try?

Joe stepped closer. "It's the only way any of us is going to get through this reasonably intact."

Lyla looked over her shoulder. Maybe he was right. Maybe risking reaching out for more was wrong, right here, right now.

"All right. As you said, I don't have much in the way of options."

Joe met her eyes, wishing there was another way. This woman had such hurt stored in her. He had such a need to heal that hurt, to shield and protect her from what the future held. He had never been so vulnerable in his life.

"Do you want to take a shower and rest here before we move you to new quarters? I'll camp out on this chair for an hour or so. Then we'll move your things to Pippa's cabin."

Lyla was past being startled at the abrupt change of topic. "Do you think that's really necessary? There is a lock on the door. As close as these cabins are there is no real chance of someone attacking me without making enough noise to raise an alarm."

"We don't know where the threat lies or how much money, if any, is being thrown out as a reward for your silence. Taking chances is definitely out. We've talked about this.

When I'm not with you, Josh and Pippa will be. I don't think even this Navaro creep is going to risk taking out two or three of us in a closed environment such as this ship. Too suspicious and no way off the boat unless we happen to be in port."

He moved to the chair and picked up the magazine on the table beside it. "Go get your shower or whatever."

Lyla shrugged, trying not to look at him as she collected her travel bag and retired to the bathroom. She had never had a roommate or a male around on a permanent basis. The prospect of having to cut her teeth on a man like Joe was daunting to say the least.

"Damn Navaro," she muttered under her breath as she stepped into the steaming cascade of water.

CHAPTER FOURTEEN

"I wonder how Joe and Lyla are making out?" Pippa asked, turning in Josh's arms. The shower warmed her back as her breasts pressed into the wall of his chest.

Josh bent his head, taking her lips with a quick nip of intent. "Not as well as I am," he teased.

Pippa's eyes danced as she rotated her hips. His groan and the sudden heat in his look were contagious.

"It is not gentlemanly to be so triumphant," she breathed, enjoying the sensation of his hair rubbing over her sensitive nipples.

"I never professed to be a gentleman. You, my gorgeous piece of woman, definitely don't fit the archaic description of a lady." He laughed at her masterpiece of a pout.

"I like that."

His hands curved around her bottom, cupping the delicious contours, lifting her higher and closer.

"So do I. More than I can tell you."

He nipped her neck, feeling the shivers that raced through her body. She was so responsive, demanding and submissive by turns. He hadn't known making love could have so many facets nor bring so much pure pleasure.

Pippa wrapped her arms around him, trusting him to keep them safely vertical. "You do feel so good," she purred, arching into his strength.

He grinned, his eyes dark with secrets he hadn't known he knew. "I'm going to feel even better."

She laughed huskily. "How?"

He bent to whisper in her ear. Pippa's expression stilled, then bloomed with curiosity and delight. "Why, Joshua Luck, I didn't know you had it in you."

"Woman, you are leaving yourself wide open," he said roughly, releasing her.

The small confines of the stall weren't scaled for what he really wanted. After flipping the shower off, he opened the door and urged Pippa out.

She pulled the clip from her hair, allowing it to rain over her damp shoulders. Then she reached for a towel, but before she could use it, Josh swept her up in his arms and carried her to the bed, dumping her in the middle. Bouncing twice, her hair flying, Pippa giggled.

"Are we starting already?"

Josh came down beside her, grabbing her before she could scoot away. "Only continuing," he replied before covering her mouth with his.

Her desire was no less volatile than his. In an instant, any thought of conversation died. Play became reality. His strength matched hers. He rolled over, taking her with him.

Pippa rose over his hips, her eyes alight with a woman's power as they joined. Her hair was a silver fall around her, teasing his chest, wrapping around him so that they were enclosed in a silky veil. Josh caught her face, staring at her features as though he would memorize each one.

"Angel or mistress?"

"Both. Neither. Only a woman."

"More. So much more." He brought her down so that their lips were but a breath away. "I could get lost in you. Drown in your passion. Fly with your laugh." His breath came out in a broken sound. "It isn't supposed to feel like this."

Pippa touched his lips, stilling the words that would demand more than she thought she had to give.

"Thirteen days, Josh. That's all we gave ourselves. Don't think of more."

"Why, Pippa?"

He searched her eyes, watching the passion die, seeing the secrets he didn't share. The secrets he now wanted to secret, to understand.

"Tell me you don't feel as I do."

"I don't lie. But I also know myself. I don't give, not the way you would need. I don't know how to bend, Josh. Or compromise." She kissed him softly. "Neither do you. For a moment, for now, we can share, but forever...how?"

"How do we know until we try?"

"Children, young fools who still believe dreams can come true, would ignore what we've both spent a lifetime becoming. We are neither. You didn't get where you are today by giving way to anyone but yourself. Your financial world is just that, your world. Just as my world is my writing. It demands everything I have to give. Not much leftover in time or attention to offer a partner for either of us."

"You would walk away from this?"

"Not easily. Not lightly and certainly not without pain, but, yes. I don't like hurting, myself or anyone else."

Her eyes held his, demanding he realize what and who she was.

"For this time, we can give to each other. I can teach you about living for the moment, and you can show me that I can be this vulnerable. I never have been, you know. We will both benefit from our time together, but that's all there is. That's all there can be. I cannot live in your world of plans, schedules, and corporate games permanently, and you would not want to live in mine, where a whim and an impulse are the only ruling forces."

Josh felt the pain of her refusal in a way that had never happened before. But mixed with the hurt was an admiration for her courage and her vision. Another woman would have listened with only her need in mind. Pippa had cared enough to see his as well. She had spoken only the truth.

"I wish I was different."

She smiled slightly, shaking her head so that her hair shimmered around them.

"I don't. I would not care for you as I do." She kissed him again, this time doing a leisurely job of it.

Josh played her game, letting the passion rise, feeling her honesty as another facet to the woman.

"Nor I you," he whispered, tasting his way to her breasts. Her gasp of pleasure shot through him. His tongue paid homage to her beauty as the afternoon gave way to early evening.

When he finally left her cabin to return to his own to dress for dinner on the island, he had never felt so invigorated, so at peace with himself and his world. He contacted Joe, smiling to himself. Joe's abrupt response dimmed his mood.

"Problems?" he asked.

"You can't possibly wear that," Pippa said decisively. She eyed the plain street-length dress with disfavor. The dark-green shade would have done for someone with a vibrant coloring but not for Lyla's more subtle tones. It hadn't taken them long to get Lyla settled in her cabin. Fortunately, the suite boasted two queen beds.

"Don't you have anything bright, cut a little low? I don't know where my mind was in not thinking of evening things for you when we were shopping."

Lyla surveyed the meager contents of her closet.

"No," she stated flatly, frowning. She didn't have anything that would compare to Pippa's lime sheath with its short skirt edged by a deep sexy flounce that trailed from waist to thigh to flirt with the slit beneath.

Pippa caught Lyla's hand to pull her across the room to another set of doors. "Come on. You and I are going shopping. This time no money involved."

Lyla tried to hold back. The idea of wearing anything from Pippa's very scantily cut wardrobe was mind boggling. She would never have that kind of self-assurance or boldness even before the mess her life currently was.

"We don't have time," she protested. "No, really, what I have will work."

"No woman should wear anything just because it works."

Pippa ignored the rumpled sheets falling off the bed where she and Josh had spent their pleasurable moments. She snapped open her closet and started pulling out dresses.

"Take off that robe and get into one of these."

Lyla dodged the froth flying at her, her mouth agape. Admittedly, she didn't know much about fashion, but even she could tell the gowns emerging from the closet were not only expensive but designer originals as well.

"Pippa, I appreciate the thought, but I can't wear..."

Pippa swung around, leveling a look that dried Lyla's protest on her lips. "You can and you will. In the first place, this restaurant that Joe is talking about is something to see.

Second, stop trying to crawl back into that shell. You're a woman who will always pay for the dressing. I don't know why you've taken on this drab habit. I can't believe that this mess you're in is completely responsible and I damn well won't ask questions.

But I will tell you this. I have no patience with waste or self-pity. The clothes are here and so am I. So are Josh and Joe. Either you stand up for yourself or you walk. I've got other things to do besides drag you around by your ear, trying to keep you alive and breathing. You want to live, then reach out and grab the moment. Wring every drop of life out of every second."

Pippa was breathing hard by the time she finished. Her hands were propped on her hips, her breasts heaving beneath the silk of her dress. Light flashed in the diamonds and peridots dangling from her ears. A crystal rose ornament tucked in the side-swept style of her hair added more fire and sparkle to her temper.

Lyla glanced at the clothes, feeling a bit like Cinderella in front of her fairy godmother. "I've never worn this kind of style," she admitted wistfully.

"From what I can tell you've never worn much of a sexy style in anything before," Pippa replied, smiling slightly. She nodded toward the serviceable robe.

Lyla sighed. "You're right, I haven't."

"Why?" She held up a hand when Lyla gave her a startled look. "I know. I said I wouldn't ask questions. So I lied."

Lyla laughed. "It's no great secret. I just didn't have the money in the beginning. Mother raised me alone. My father, in his infinite wisdom, never paid a penny of child support so there just wasn't enough in our house to go around and I desperately wanted to go to college.

Besides, I was plain, a little brainy but plain. I didn't date. I didn't have time. Working every moment I wasn't studying was the only way I could stay in school. Then when I was done and I got into the job market, again I didn't have the resources to outfit myself nor did I have the knowledge."

She looked down at the clothes on the bed. "When I finally started to pull out of the hole the arrest came. Then I didn't care. All I wanted to do was hide."

"Well, no more," Pippa said briskly. She dropped into a chair waving Lyla toward the bathroom. "Change. We don't have much time and we still have to do your makeup. It's a good thing our skin tones are so similar."

Lyla glanced at Pippa, reading the purpose in her eyes and the challenge. The same imp that had prompted her to buy and wear the skimpy shorts and top raised its head again. She glanced at the lovely gowns.

"Which do you think?"

"The rose," Pippa said promptly. "What size are your feet?"

Past being startled or even worried, Lyla told her. First Joe then Pippa had demanded she take charge of her own life. It was time she did, she decided as she shrugged out of her robe.

From this moment on, no matter what happened or how much she wanted to hide, she wasn't going to do it. Reaching out to life, not running from it, was going to be her guiding force.

"We're in luck. We're the enough to the same size except in the bust. You are more delicate there than I am."

She watched critically as Lyla wiggled into the pink slip style dress. The color instantly brought a glow to Lyla's hair, eyes, and skin. The figure-hugging style clung lightly in all the right places, making the most of her slender shape and gentle curves.

The keyhole neckline was discreetly sexy and the only real detailing on the gown. Pippa got up, diving back into her closet to emerge, without a hair out of place, with a pair of matching slippers dangling from her fingers.

"Now get these on and we'll work magic with the wonders of the cosmetic world."

Laughing, feeling marvelously alive, Lyla took the shoes. As she slipped her feet into the dainty straps, she wondered what Joe would make of the new her. Surely a friend could admire another friend. Just maybe that friend might discover that distance was not the answer after all.

"You look like the devil." Josh surveyed his brother critically.

"And you look like you've lost ten years since this afternoon," Joe replied as he shrugged into his shirt. "Pippa wouldn't be wearing that same look by any chance, would she?"

Josh grinned, the memories of the time with Pippa adding depth to the usual cold darkness of his eyes. Leaning back in his chair, he said, "Don't try to change the subject. What's going on between you and Lyla? You're wound tighter than a spring."

Joe glanced at Josh, surprised to discover his expression was more perceptive than shrewd. It was almost impossible to believe this was the same hard bitten corporate executive who had boarded the ship the day before.

When Joe didn't speak, Josh prompted, "I realize I'm rather late in developing any brotherly tendencies, but if you need an ear, I'll be glad to listen."

Joe sighed as he raked his fingers through his hair. The restless gesture was as unusual for him as Josh's offer.

"I don't know what's wrong with me," he admitted finally. "I'm so accustomed to being at peace with myself and the world I have chosen. It's been years since I've let myself be vulnerable. Lyla makes me vulnerable and the damnable part is she doesn't seem to know it."

Josh frowned, hearing the very real confusion in his brother's voice. "With the baggage she's carrying, I'm surprised she knows what day it is. Just when she was beginning to relax that damn Donovan shows up. If Pippa hadn't drawn her out, I doubt I would have even noticed she was on the ship in spite of the fact that her cabin is no more than six down from Pippa's and mine. She has a way of disappearing into the scenery. Keeping that kind of low profile had its uses but it also means she is not that aware of the people around her."

Anger, swift and unexpected, lit Joe's eyes. "I wouldn't go that far," he replied irritably.

Josh's lips twitched at the barely suppressed emotion. "I didn't say she isn't pretty. I think she could be if she'd stop hiding behind every potted plant in town. Nor do I think her uncaring. But, Joe, she is very unaware right now."

Joe took a hasty step toward Josh. Suddenly he laughed and flung himself down in a chair. "Cute, big brother, really cute. "

"Well, at least we've established why you're feeling vulnerable. Having been dealt the same shocker of a hand, I can sympathize with the feeling. Pippa makes me feel like a damn fool, too cautious for my own good and younger than the gray in my hair tells me I am."

Joe's comment was pithy and short. Josh laughed, genuinely amused at his vehemence.

"What are you going to do about Lyla?"

"I don't like being used."

Josh's brows rose at the abrupt announcement.

169

"If there was a picture of a woman who is a user it wouldn't be Lyla. I doubt she has that kind of hardness."

"I didn't say she knew she was using me."

"Then what did you say?"

"Lyla isn't like Pippa."

"Thank God for that," Josh said fervently.

Joe laughed, then quickly sobered.

"She isn't very experienced. You were right about that, and with this trial thing and the way everyone has responded to her involvement, her life just stopped around twenty-four when the whole mess began four years ago.

Then the three of us came along. We believe her. You and Pippa are obviously involved, and I made the mistake of letting her see that I find her attractive."

The sight of Josh's skeptical expression made him amend the last statement. "All right, more than attractive. Something about her gets into my mind. I want to keep her safe. Right the world." He grimaced at his own flights of fantasy. "Stupid, isn't it?"

Josh didn't answer immediately. Joe's response to Lyla matched the depth of his own to Pippa. Because of his newly awakening emotions, because of the sensitivity he was learning from Pippa, he thought beyond the facts.

"It isn't stupid. Lyla needs help. We all agree on that. You are a man who has made his life working with and in the emotions, minds, and hearts of others. You are far more likely to feel for her. It could be that."

"Don't you think I haven't considered that possibility?"

"And?"

Joe met his eyes, his own dark with an angry intensity. "I know those symptoms. This is different."

"She doesn't feel the same?"

His mouth tightened. "Oh, that's the beauty of the jest," he murmured bitterly. "She feels exactly the same. Or thinks she does.

But in the next breath she tells me how grateful she is that I know, because of my gift, she isn't guilty and how wonderful it is not to be alone anymore. You and Pippa just took it on faith or intuition. I know because I can see into her mind."

This time it was Josh's oath that sliced the silence with sound.

"Exactly. I can't back off without leaving her at the mercy of whoever is out there waiting for her and I damn well can't take her to my bed like I really want to do. I won't be a prop, feeling the way I do. I am not into emotional suicide."

"There is a way out that we haven't talked about. Both of us could afford to hire her a bodyguard."

"Even if she would agree to that, which I doubt, a bodyguard wouldn't necessarily guarantee her safety."

"We aren't offering any guarantees, either. Besides. what happens when this cruise is over? Not once have any of us thought of that."

Joe turned away to pull on his jacket. "I don't know. I'm beginning to think I don't know anything."

Josh rose and moved to his side. "You could just relax and let the chips fall as they will."

Joe shot him a look, half irritated and half amused. "You have definitely changed. I didn't think you ever waited anything out."

"No, I never have. But that doesn't mean I was right. If this trip has taught me anything, it's that some things just aren't meant to be grabbed. Patience and finesse have a lot going for them."

The two men walked to the door. "You've got the fastest patience I've ever seen if you and Pippa are any example."

Josh tipped back his head, laughing. "Yes, but you must remember, I'm new at this and so is Pippa. We're both used to getting what we want when we want it. Bone-selfish, she calls it. I'm inclined to agree."

"Selfish people would not have stepped in for Lyla," Joe pointed out as they left the cabin and turned two corners to bring them to Pippa's corridor.

"Pippa stepped, I got dragged."

"Did I hear my name mentioned?" Pippa demanded, opening the door of her cabin just as the men arrived.

Josh moved into the room, his eyes only for her. Taking Pippa in his arms, he kissed her deeply. One hour was too much time to give away when they had so few days left together. He didn't hear Joe's startled murmur as he caught sight of the new Lyla.

Joe passed the embracing pair, his gaze slipping over Lyla as she stood frozen before him.

"Do you like it?" Lyla asked when he didn't speak.

Joe nodded, not even realizing that he was responding. "I don't remember this when we were shopping."

There was no way he couldn't have missed the way she looked, all long limbs and elegant lines. The curves of her body tantalized him, drawing a response with every breath she drew. The mystery of her demanded his attention, his touch. It was all he could do to keep his hands at his sides.

Lyla looked down at the shimmering fabric that flowed over her skin. As soft as a kiss and as exciting at the sizzle of a storm in the air,

"Pippa. It's her dress and her makeup," she said softly, looking up at him. For a moment, she couldn't have moved if she had been facing danger. His eyes held an intensity, questions that she so wanted to answer. No matter what had brought them to this moment, she desired him more than she had ever wanted any man in her life.

The metamorphosis was incredible, not just the clothes and cosmetics but the change in Lyla herself. Lyla was so different. Even her voice had changed. It was huskier, softer, more an invitation than a recitation of information.

Her eyes shone with secrets that had been whispered in the Garden of Eden. Her body was perfect, slender, made for his hands. His fingers itched to touch the flower-soft skin that the dress embraced. Her hair was a rippling fall of cinnamon silk. The light seemed to dance in the delicate strands, teasing him almost as much as the exotic scent she wore.

Josh raised his head, smiling into Pippa's pale eyes. "I needed that," he whispered.

"So did I," she murmured softly, touching his cheek. "But if we don't stop now, we might embarrass our other half."

He grinned, too delighted with his world at the moment to care. "Joe's old enough. He should know about sex by now."

Pippa batted her lashes, her lips curving into a smile he distinctly remembered.

"Behave, woman," he commanded, sliding his hand down her length to tap her on the bottom. Her wiggle against his fingers slipped another notch free of his restraint.

He groaned, "I am not an exhibitionist." He set her from him.

"Okay," Pippa agreed blithely. "Behold our handiwork," she added, her voice no longer seductive to the point of madness.

Josh glanced at Lyla then did a double take. "Lyla?" he said before he thought.

Lyla started, smiling hesitantly. "It's me."

"It is definitely you," he agreed, giving her an uncomplicated smile of admiration.

Lyla let out her breath in a long sigh. "You don't think I look odd."

"Beautiful," he corrected. "Joe and I are going to be facing some serious male envy tonight. Maybe we should have worn body armor."

Lyla eyes lit with the compliment. She was aware that Joe had said little, only looked stunned. Although she was glad that Josh seemed to have dropped his earlier coldness, it was Joe's approval she really wanted.

"If you're going to stand there gaping all night, we'll be late to dinner," Josh prompted, trying not to smile at Joe's amazement.

Joe nodded, forcing his mind to function. "You are beautiful," he said stiffly.

When Lyla had been nothing special to look at, he had been attracted to her. This delicately exquisite creature was something even more dangerous. His control and perspective had never been harder to achieve. Forget peace. With Lyla around, he might never achieve that nirvana again.

He turned to Pippa, needing a diversion. "You did a wonderful job," he said sincerely.

Lyla's face lost some of its animation at the compliment and the rider. Josh frowned slightly. Even as a child, Joe had been too gentle to knowingly cause pain to another.

"All the paint and glitz in the world can only highlight what already exists," Pippa said flatly, wondering what was wrong with Joe. She would have thought he had more finesse than he was currently displaying.

It hadn't occurred to her that he wouldn't like the changes in Lyla. She couldn't have been mistaken about his interest. She looked at Josh, finding him watching his brother intently. Confused, but determined not to spoil the evening for Lyla, she tucked one hand into the crook of Josh's arm and the other into Lyla's.

"I don't know about the rest of you, but I'm starving. Let's go."

CHAPTER FIFTEEN

Josh stared down at Pippa's face as she lay sleeping beside him. The situation with Donovan had created a real problem in sleeping arrangements that first night. He hadn't wanted to give up having Pippa in his bed.

She had been adamant about Lyla not being alone. Pippa had the only suite with two beds. Joe had a small cabin since he was part of the staff, guest status though it was. No extra space.

By the end of dinner and a lot of discussion, Lyla had agreed to remain in Pippa's cabin with Joe taking Pippa's bed as a safeguard so that Pippa could share Josh's cabin.

He smiled in the early morning light as he remembered the lively discussion of his sex life and the way to facilitate it by the woman lying so innocently asleep beside him. Watching his younger brother coping with Pippa's remarks and Lyla's unequal struggle to avoid coming between Pippa and her pleasures tickled a laugh to start the day.

He shifted to his side, still smiling as he touched Pippa's cheek lightly with a forefinger.

How she could look so like an angel when she had such a Machiavellian mind was part of the mystery and the paradox of the woman. The need for her should have eased some these last five days of having her at night and enjoying the novelty of being with her, then Joe and Lyla by day.

He was closer to Joe than he had been in years. A good part of that growing relationship was due to Pippa's light hand and impossible to resist enjoyment of life in all its guises. The four of them spent time together when Joe's schedule allowed. Lyla spent time backstage, well protected by the crew while Joe did his work.

Lyla was blooming in spite of having Donovan hanging around like a dark cloud. He hadn't approached Lyla directly again. As far as Josh could determine, the man was confining his activities to standing guard. If the captain knew anything about the situation, Joe had not been able confirm it.

At that moment, Pippa stretched as she opened her eyes and smiled drowsily. "Good morning."

He settled her closer. So little time and so much living to cram into the hours left. He breathed in her scent, remembering the passion of the night and the quiet that had come after.

Pippa snuggled nearer, delighting in the way Josh liked to hold her. She wouldn't have thought of him as a tactile person. But he was with her. Her hands smoothed over his body, stroking the firm muscles as she let the morning sink into her mind. This was the best part of the day. A long, slow climb into reality in the arms of a man who made exquisite love.

"I'm glad I came on this cruise," she whispered.

Josh closed his eyes at the words. He didn't need the reminder of how little time remained to them. With effort he kept his voice from betraying his need for a more lasting promise.

"I'm glad too."

Pippa rolled onto Josh's chest and pillowed her hands under her chin. As her mind began to function, she realized something was bothering Josh. She thought she knew what. She touched the lines on his brow, smoothing the creasing gently.

"It's Joe, isn't it? You are seeing the same thing I am. They are attracted to each other, but they are holding back. Her situation is complicated. Both of them could get hurt in more ways than one.

Add that damn Donovan following us around for the last five days. He might as well hang out a sign. Here's Lyla Carson, folks," she added in deep disgust.

Josh stroked her back, his eyes for once not fixed on her face. To look at her was to toss caution to the sky and say things that would tear apart the dream they shared.

"Joe's having a hard time of it. I'm fairly certain he's falling in love with our little Lyla."

Pippa inhaled deeply, her breasts settling more comfortably against Josh's chest. "Well, that at least is a step in the right direction because I think she's up to her eyebrows deep in love with him. He has to be blind not to know it."

"It's only been five days," he reminded her. "Joe doesn't move that fast emotionally. His gift makes that risky."

He sighed deeply. "Lyla's situation is a very real complication. I don't think he trusts himself or her because of it."

Pippa frowned, disturbed at the flat tone and the way he was avoiding her eyes. "So have an affair. Maybe they will find that neither of them wants more. Self-denial isn't doing anything but making both of them edgy."

"I can't see Lyla choosing that path. Can you? Besides, I can't see Joe thinking of Lyla that way. Neither of them is like us about marriage and commitment."

Even as he said the words that had once been true on his side, he wished he hadn't.

Pippa missed the change in his tone, her mind more on the man than the words she had understood from the first. She touched his lips, smiling at his question.

"No, I can't imagine either of them choosing our way. Lyla is made for home, work she loves, a man to love and, when the timing's right, children. Joe needs a woman who understands what he does but still treats him as a man not a psychic. He needs the normal to counterbalance his gift. Lyla could give him that."

She sighed at the picture she had verbally drawn. Pretty and predictable. Not for her.

"We like our freedom. I like knowing I don't have to worry about thinking of a way to avoid a proposal or proposition I don't want from a man I happen to think is sexier than sin."

Expecting his grin, she was surprised at the tension suddenly stiffening his body, something akin to pain in his eyes.

"Josh?" she said, stroking his face. Uneasy, disturbed at the abrupt change in the atmosphere, she waited.

"I love you, Pippa." Josh watched her eyes widen, saw the moment when she tried to force the words from her mind.

Two days ago, he had finally realized what the emotion that had been growing steadily stronger really was. Love. He had been as surprised then as she looked now. He hadn't intended to tell her. She had certainly made her stand clear. But lying had never been his strength.

"I know we make beautiful love together, but that isn't the same. I don't need pretty words and implied promises," Pippa tried to reason. Love is a small word for a life changing upheaval

Josh cradled her face in his palms. "I didn't want to. I was no more interested in changing my life to fit someone else than you were. But the simple truth is that these last few days have been the best of my life. Is it right that we only have eight left out of the future? I'm selfish enough to want more."

There were few times in her life when Pippa was at a loss for words. This ranked as number one.

"Think about it, Pippa. Do you really want to spend the rest of your life alone? Getting your emotional support from nieces and nephews who have their own lives, their own loves?

What kind of a life will that be for you? You'll be alone, dependent on others. If you're sick and they have commitments, will you be able to call them to you?"

He shook her once. Her hair spilled around them. "I know you. You wouldn't take from them no matter how great your own need."

Pippa stared into his eyes, seeing a future she had accepted but refused to dwell on written there.

"Don't do this to us. There is so little time," she murmured, pleading as she never had in her life.

"There is all the time you want if you would just reach out and take it."

Pippa tried to pull away. Thinking rationally when he held her was impossible. "You don't know what I'm like when I'm working. You have only seen me like this."

Josh rolled over, trapping her beneath him. "Excuses! Coward, Pippa?" The challenge was thrown in a hard voice. Josh glared down at her, in no mood to be kind to either of them.

Pippa stared back, her eyes flashing with blue fire. Anger was a lash for him and the future he tried to dangle before her.

"Damn you. You will not win that way. Think what you like."

"You won't even try. What would you have me think?"

"I told you I did try."

"Tell me you don't love me."

"I do love you, but that isn't enough. If I was a fool or too young to realize life has little kindness for love, I would fall into your arms and vow to be your other half for always." Her hands dug into his shoulders.

Josh didn't notice the pain of her hold, only of her words. Her strength had always held his admiration. Now it was the spear delivering the killing blow to his hopes. There was no yielding in her, no room for a compromise he would have been willing to make.

He, who never compromised for anyone, had been prepared to bend for this woman. Frustration cut the leash of his temper. He rolled off her, giving her his back as he got to his feet and dragged on a robe.

"Then go, damn you. Walk away from the best thing that has ever happened to either one of us. Stay in that sterile, carefully ordered world of yours. Live for a few moments with someone who cares and then walk away."

He turned, his eyes catching and holding her prisoner as she lay on the bed, naked, before him.

"Walk alone into the sunset. But remember this. I loved you and would have shared more with you than I have ever shared with anyone. Remember what you gave me.

Trust, a commodity you rarely offer. Love, something you know as little about as I. And need. That's what scares you, Phillippa. Need. I need you. I'm not afraid to say it, but you are."

He watched her for one moment. When she only looked back at him, her face as smooth as the early morning sea, he turned from her and headed for the bath.

"If you have any kindness in you at all, be gone when I come out." He heard the bed rustle slightly. He paused with his hand on the door.

"I'll keep up my end of the pact to protect Lyla. I gave my word. But we end here." He opened the panel, walked in, and closed the wood between them.

Pippa stared at the door, feeling as though she was moving through a kind of fog. Shock, she thought as she lifted her hands and watched them tremble. So much emotion. A few days ago, neither she nor Josh would have been so open with each other. He was right about some things.

But not about their future. She rose, frowning slightly as she looked around for her robe. Josh wanted her gone and gone she would be. It wasn't until she was back in her own cabin, thankfully empty of Lyla's presence for the moment, that she began to surface. Reality was a cold place when she thought of the last days of the trip. To meet Josh, to know that the nights wouldn't have his warmth and passion, was a cruel punishment for crimes she hadn't known she committed.

But the alternative was worse. At least this way the break was swift and clean. To live and love with Josh in the real world would be as slow death for them. She loved him too much and knew herself too well to take the risk.

Fort-de-France, Martinique, arose out of the sea as a rugged, almost forbidding landscape of rock. Pippa stood at the rail, watching the ship move closer to their next destination. The dawn was just breaking, offering enough light to see. The morning was gentle, a soft breeze on the skin, a hint of the warmth of the day to come.

She sighed, wishing the cruise was at an end. The thought of repeating the last two days was a shroud of darkness and futility on her personal horizon. Lyla and Joe were so polite that any conversation was almost an exercise in etiquette.

Josh had reverted to his taciturn self, answering only when absolutely necessary. Sightseeing had been more a technical maneuver than an enjoyable outing that first day after her quarrel with Josh.

Even dinner, delightful though the restaurants had been, had done nothing to soften Josh's attitude. And yesterday they had been at sea, in short, imprisoned on the ship. The only redeeming feature had been that Lyla was relatively safe in the closed environment.

"You couldn't sleep either?" Joe murmured, joining Pippa at the rail.

She looked at him out of the corner of her eye. "No." He appeared no more rested than she felt.

Joe stared at the island growing larger with each lift of a wave. "I'd offer to help, but I seem to be doing no better with the situation." He gripped the metal beneath his palms.

Pippa turned, touching his hands, feeling his tension. "Forget my problems. The end of this trip will see them resolved. No one has made a move on Lyla. Donovan is acting more like a passenger than a bodyguard."

He studied her, shaking his head. "I wasn't thinking about that. I'm talking about you and my brother. That isn't going away when the cruise is over. You're fighting a losing battle."

Pippa managed a smile, a constrained effort but better than nothing." No, I'm not. Josh is as stubborn as I. A relationship between us would be more damaging than this."

"Making judgments, especially judgments about the future, is never a good idea."

"This from a man who makes his living looking beyond the present?" Her brows rose, her eyes lightly mocking. "Your situation with Lyla isn't doing much better."

He grimaced. "Who better to know how changeable time and knowledge can make one?"

"What about Lyla?"

Joe shrugged, wishing Pippa hadn't asked. "What about her?" he replied, trying for time.

"Don't be obtuse. What do you see for her? Have we done the right thing?"

"It isn't a question of right. It's a question of only." He glanced away then.

"The four of us are tied together. That much I can see clearly. But before this trip is over, the tie will either be severed or fused so perfectly that no break or fusion will ever be possible again."

Pippa said nothing for a moment as she absorbed the prophecy. "All four of us?"

He inclined his head. "I am the only one who came on this trip through planning. Each of you followed an impulse. Yet every one of us had to be here at this place, in this time. Our lives have been leading to this moment."

Pippa took a step away. Joe's lips twisted at the gesture. "Unnerving, isn't it?" He released his grip on the rail and half turned.

"All my life I've had access to information that frightened and repelled even as it fascinated. I haven't touched Lyla. It is killing me to keep my distance.

Lyla is in love with me and I with her, but I can't ask her to accept what I am and what it will mean in our lives. She thinks she understands but she hasn't had to live with this gift day after day. Seeing things, knowing things and more often than not unable to do anything about what that knowing might mean.

It isn't my right to provide answers just because I have them. Everyone has a right to make his or her choice. I have to wait to be asked. Even the simplest friendships are minefields of problems. Sometimes I don't even want to try anymore."

Pippa closed her eyes on the blind despair in his admission. Lorelei and even Jason had known such emptiness and at such a cost. She had found the words for them. She could do no less for this man with the gentle eyes and older-than-time-itself soul. Opening her lashes, she moved to his side, taking his hand.

"I can't see the future, but I can tell you this. When someone is as damaged as Lyla, if they survive, they are stronger than anyone can imagine. It's almost as if the ability to be really hurt has been burned right out of them.

They have a tremendous capacity to love, to offer all of themselves rather than less. But only to one who has earned or gained their trust. For that person they will lay down their life without counting the cost.

That is Lyla's legacy. I think, she, more than anyone, can handle what you are and what you must be. In return you can give her what no one else can. You know she did not do the things she was accused of. The rest of us can only believe she didn't, and, in her mind, that will never be enough. So, you see, your power is a gift to her, not the burden you imagine."

Joe stared into Pippa's eyes, finding the path to the truth in the sky-blue depths. Strength seemed to flow from her to him through their joined hands. His doubts fell away, tension ebbing from his body as though it had never been. He felt renewed. His hand turned in hers, returning the pressure.

"One day I hope you realize how much you really do see." He bent his head, his lips touching her forehead, her cheek. "You are one special woman, Pippa Weldon. I am happier than I can say that you took me and Lyla into your heart."

Pippa smiled, releasing his hand and stepping back. This time her gesture brought no pain. "You're going to her?"

"As fast as these legs will carry me."

"You'll have a fight on your hands."

"I know. She'll be afraid her past will always taint our lives. But I'll win in the end."

"I'm counting on it. She's in my suite. I'll be browsing the boutiques for a while. You'll have the place to yourselves if you're interested."

He grinned as he walked away. Josh was crazy if he didn't find a way to marry Pippa.

Josh stood in the shadow of the deck, watching his brother and Pippa. Jealousy, an emotion with which he had no acquaintance, surged through him. His hands clenched at his sides as he fought the urge to stalk over to the pair and snatch them apart.

Then as he watched, he did more than look. He began to really see. Joe was hurting, and somehow Pippa was healing his pain. His fingers unclenched as his body relaxed. Jealousy turned to curiosity then to pride as he saw Joe change.

His brother's face held such peace in the end, such strength of purpose that Josh could not help being impressed. He saw Joe kiss Pippa and then walk away.

He should have turned away. For as soon as Pippa thought herself unobserved, her calm expression broke. Pain such as he hoped never to see again frayed the edges of her composure. Her body was stiff, refusing to surrender even as she turned to look out to the sea. Without realizing that he had moved, Josh joined her, slipping his arms around her to pull her against his chest.

Pippa resisted the first touch. "Don't, Josh," she whispered, tears she didn't want him to witness blurring her eyes.

"I will, Pippa. I don't know what's wrong, but you need me. You don't have to say anything but let me hold you until you don't hurt anymore."

The tears overflowed and slipped down her cheeks, silent streams of grief and loss. His arms around her were all her dreams and her nightmares. Her body softened, yielding to his.

Josh rested his chin on her hair, sighing gently. She was so slight in his embrace, a package of dynamite that one could easily fit into a pocket.

The sun rose, the island evolved into a bustling dock, and the noise of civilization. No words were spoken between them. Pippa's tears dried. Josh knew it was time to release her. For one instant he succumbed to the temptation of her in his arms. He pressed his lips to her bright hair then let her go.

Pippa turned, not sure how to thank him. She needn't have worried. He was yards away, his stride that elegant walk that she loved so much, widening the distance between them with every step. He was giving her what she wanted, and she hated it.

"Why couldn't I have loved a man who fit into my niche?" she whispered to the morning.

CHAPTER SIXTEEN

Joe hesitated at the door of Pippa's cabin. Talking to Pippa had given him the kick in the courage he needed. But faced with the fact of what he wanted to do, he paused.

What if he was wrong? His lips curved faintly as the thought intruded. Love was reputed to make fools of brave men. His hand descended. Almost as though she was waiting for him, Lyla opened the door.

"I came for you," he said, looking at her, making no effort to step across the threshold.

Lyla stared into his dark eyes, seeing a new light in the still depths. "Why?"

"I care about you. I want a chance to explore what we can be together." The words were stark because he had no pretty speeches to explain how important she was to him.

Lyla moved back, gesturing him inside. "Why now? You made it clear enough a few days ago that anything between us wasn't possible."

She thought about the nights she had lain in bed, staring out into the black satin sky sprinkled with diamond stars. Alone but very aware of him sleeping in the bed across from hers, his breathing almost matching the rhythm of her heart.

She had learned the word *alone* had more dimensions than she had guessed. Silence. No longer a friend she had hoped to have around her forever. Solitude, no more the state to which she had aspired. Joe had taught her that all three were the worst kind of existence.

Joe closed the door behind him and locked it. He knew then that just telling her how he felt would not be enough. Her pain went too deep, and her fear was no small piece of her personality.

"I was afraid." He smiled grimly when her head snapped around, her eyes wide with surprise.

"You aren't the only one who can have doubts. I am no more interested in being hurt than you. Love makes all of us feel as though our heads are on the chopping block."

Lyla searched his expression, wanting to believe. "You believed I was using you." The thought still stung even now, after she realized why and how he had made such a judgement.

"But I never thought you were consciously using me," he argued, taking a step closer. He wanted to have her in his arms, but he knew that he had to reach her mind before he possessed her body.

"What do you want of me?" she whispered.

"Your hand in mine. Time to share, to learn of each other without the doubts creeping into destroy us before we begin." Another step and he was only a few inches away.

Lyla lifted her hand touching his chest, feeling his heart beat beneath her palm.

"Being with you would have been hard for me even before this mess with the appeal. Then Donovan following us around. The threat of

Navaro waiting to eliminate me. I feel like I'm on a merry-go-round that keeps spinning faster and faster, totally out of my control.

I want to hold on to you so that I won't go flying off the edge of the world. Maybe you were right. Maybe I am using you." Because he was honest, she could be no less.

He covered her fingers with his and raised his free hand to her cheek. "Maybe you are. Or maybe I'm using you. Or perhaps this is what caring is all about. When one is weak the other is strong."

She smiled a little, lighter for his understanding. "I want to try," she admitted huskily. "I really want to try."

He pulled her close, fitting her body to his. "That, pretty lady, is the best news I've ever heard."

She lifted her face, her eyes warming with desire. He bent his head, nibbling at her lips. "Do you have any idea how hard it has been sharing this cabin with you, knowing you were sleeping so close and yet so far away?"

Her courage in hand, she whispered, "Do you have any idea how hard it was to pretend to sleep with you in this room and the door locking the world outside?"

His arms tightened around her. "How badly do you want to see Fort-de-France?"

"Not much," she murmured, inhaling his scent even as she moved nearer. She gasped softly as his lips settled at the base of her neck. Delicious shivers brought chills that demanded she curl into his heat.

"Good," he whispered against her skin, his tongue flicking out to trace the creamy flesh with random patterns. "I have a much better itinerary for the day."

Lyla tipped back her head, her lashes fanning shut. "Do you?"

Joe lifted her in his arms and carried her to his bed. "Oh, yes." He came down beside her, his hand stroking her length through the pale lemon robe. When she moved beneath his hand he smiled. "We are going to make beautiful love to each other."

She opened her eyes, studying his expression, a sudden doubt banking the fire within. "Don't expect too much."

He touched her lips with his forefinger. "I expect nothing. We will learn together. I promise. No past for either of us. Only now, this moment, together." He leaned down, taking her mouth, showing her without words exactly what he meant.

The bold move caught Lyla off guard. Before she could worry his lips were there, his tongue gently showing her how to play, to enjoy loving. His hands touched her, sliding the robe from her shoulders.

Her skin had never felt so alive, so beautiful. Her lashes drifted shut, darkness cloaking the brightness of the morning. Her fingers traced his face, learning the contours as a blind woman would Braille. He was all heat and supple muscles. His body never trapped, only shielded her. Her legs shifted, her hips lifting as the slow tension built. The air was cool on her bare flesh, but the fire only raged higher.

Lyla opened her eyes, staring into his face as he rose above her. The intense, focused hunger in his eyes overshadowed the serenity that usually shone there.

He was waiting for her, she realized. His expression, the moisture beaded on his flesh, told of the toll his choice was taking.

Suddenly, she didn't want a gentle lover. She wanted his fire, to burn in his arms as she had never burned in any man's. Slipping her arms about his neck, she pulled him down to her as, at the same time, she lifted to him. In one thrust, two became one.

"You are beautiful," Joe groaned against her ear.

"So are you," she moaned, feeling him fill her completely.

Joe moved slowly, letting her grow accustomed to his size. He was no small man, and she was a delicately built woman.

Lyla touched his face. "Stop treating me as though I will break. I promise you I will not."

"Won't you?" He flexed.

She smiled and returned the pressure with a rotation of her hips.

"Daring me, lover?"

Lyla hadn't known it was possible to tease and laugh at this kind of moment. "Yes, I think I am," she murmured.

"Not smart." This time he moved deliberately out, hovering on the edge of complete withdrawal.

Lyla pouted up at him. "You wouldn't." His smoldering look was a giveaway.

Joe laughed softly as he slid back home. He dipped his head, taking her lips. "No, I'm too hungry to be so stupid."

Lyla wrapped her arms around him, deciding it was time this woman tried a few moves of her own. Taking him by surprise, she covered his mouth as she lifted once more. The rhythm was easy, for he met her halfway.

The fire was waiting, the need to burn urgent enough to blot out everything but the sight of the flames dancing just out of reach. Joe matched her move for move, always there, always touching as they began the swift ascent to fulfillment.

The moment came in a rush of feeling. A twin cries of need and possession rose together to shatter time with the mutual claiming. Then silence and stillness wrapped around them. Lyla opened her eyes to find Joe looking at her as though he had never seen her before.

"Those in your past were fools. You are a prize that a smart man would fight to hold."

She smiled softly, suddenly sleepy. "Only for you," she whispered as she let slumber capture her.

Joe touched her lips as he felt her relax completely. Settling her in his arms, he pulled the covers over them. The nights had been long, lonely, and restless. Having the freedom to sleep with Lyla was the thing he wanted the most at this moment.

Josh stared at the note from Joe he had found when he had returned to his cabin.

"If Lyla and I don't meet you at the gangplank by nine, don't bother looking for us. We will be making plans of our own. If you and Pippa are interested, let's have dinner tonight at Tiffany's. One of the best restaurants in the Caribbean."

Dropping the paper on the desk Josh looked out the window. "Well, little brother, you threw me a curve this time. Letting Pippa loose on an unsuspecting island is not possible and spending the day with her alone is going to be the kind of torture only a fool would knowingly inflict on himself."

He headed for the shower. "I'm a fool."

Pippa gave Joe and Lyla three hours of alone time while she shopped the ships boutiques, an occupation she usually found fun. Instead, it had been an effort to find an outfit and shoes she liked. Finally, bored with killing time, she had taken the precaution of calling Lyla's cell first before returning to her suite. The younger couple had already left the cabin and had been having a drink near the pool before going ashore to explore.

She had returned to her suite to change into one of her new purchases, hoping to change her mood. She slipped into the jungle-printed halter dress she had bought on a whim. The tie at the neck left her arms and most of her back bare, matching her bare legs.

Tan sandals and bright-green earrings completed the look. In no mood to take the time to braid her hair, she left it loose.

As she stared at her reflection in the mirror, she really looked at her image. The pensive expression on her face was new. It had been years since she had agonized over anything or anyone.

But Josh wasn't just anyone. His words, as much as she tried to deny them, had found fertile mental ground. Admitting cowardice to one's self was not an uplifting experience, she thought with a wry grimace. Not that she was going to do anything about it. Turning away with something of a flounce, she picked up her handbag and left the cabin. As she stepped into the corridor, Josh opened his door. Their eyes met.

"Perfect timing," she said for something to fill the silence.

Josh ignored the comment as he joined her. He handed her Joe's note and waited while she read it. He didn't know if he hoped she would refuse to accompany him in exploring the island or if he wanted her company. Her scent drew him closer, reminding him of all that had gone before. Why couldn't she have looked as frayed around the edges as he felt?

Pippa stared at the note, unknowingly echoing Josh's thoughts. Finally, her usual savoir faire deserting her, she lifted her eyes to his.

"Well. what do we do?"

He handed her back the hot potato, his glance mocking her attempt to put the responsibility in his lap.

"It's up to you."

She glared, in no mood for games. Saying as much, she added, "This is ridiculous. You go your way and I'll go mine."

"Afraid?" he demanded, almost angrily.

"Yes," she said baldly.

Josh stared at her. He hadn't expected her to admit it. Her honesty disarmed his temper. He caught her hand.

"Come on. If I can handle it, you can."

Caught off guard, Pippa let herself be pulled a few feet before she threw her weight against his forward progress. Josh came up short.

"I will not be dragged around like some sort of an appendage."

"Then walk. There is a lot to see, and we might as well see it together." His look challenged her.

She scowled, realizing that she didn't want to be alone with her thoughts." I suppose it is better to wander with someone rather than alone. I will go with you."

"A concession, oh queen." He dipped his head, the gesture and the tone a mockery.

Pippa kept a tight hold on her temper. Her smile was a gentle knife in the ribs, driving for the heart.

"One must be kind to the peasants, after all."

She flicked her skirt and took a step to bring her to his side. "I hope you know where you're going."

"Afraid of getting lost with me?"

They started down the hall. "I would prefer the ship and my luggage didn't leave without me."

Josh gave her a look but didn't retaliate. Instead, he turned his attention to getting them to the nearest car rental agency. When he had secured a small car, Pippa took her place beside him, a map of the island in her hand.

"Have you decided where you would like to go?"

Josh glanced at her.

Pippa stared at the lines and cities spread before her. Her mind wasn't on her task. "Does it have to be like this?"

He didn't pretend to misunderstand. "You made the choice. It wasn't mine."

Pippa raised her eyes to his. "On the deck this morning, you were different."

Josh stared at the traffic, shrugging. "A momentary lapse. Don't worry about it."

Pippa studied his closed expression, wishing she could reach him and afraid of what she would feel if she did.

"Couldn't we be friends?"

He shot her a look of acute dislike. "Is that what you do with the men who try to get too close? Turn them into eunuch-type friends?"

"That's a filthy thing to say. What's wrong with having friends?" she demanded furiously.

"Nothing, if it isn't a defense against getting involved."

"Look who's talking about involvement. I distinctly remember a certain woman named Lisa. Better a eunuch than a marble statue. The only thing that woman is good for is a bird perch."

Josh laughed before he could stop himself. "I wish I dared to tell her you said that."

Pippa's lips twitched. She turned her head, determined not to give in to his amusement.

Josh slanted her a glance. In that moment the world settled around him. He knew what he had to do.

"You might as well laugh. This day isn't going to improve until both of us start acting our age."

Pippa's chin whipped around, raising at the gleam in his eyes. "How much of my age do you want me to act?" she asked dangerously.

He grinned, relaxing. "I'd say about twenty should do it."

She shook her head, trying to stay solemn and failing. "Damn you. I wish I had never told you how much I hate being called aunt. The thought of turning into a great-aunt gives me visions of lace caps and knitting needles."

Josh's laughter was rich and uninhibited. He parked the car, still chuckling. "Honey, you couldn't knit on your best day."

"What do you mean by that? I can do anything if I bend my mind to it."

He pulled her out of the car, ignoring the people on the street to haul her close. He dropped a kiss on her nose and flicked her cheek, both maneuvers he knew would nip at her temper. The fire in her eyes promised retribution he ached to face.

He would have her, this elusive woman he loved. He would have her because no one could keep her on her toes better than he. His mistake had been trying to win her heart before he touched the flame of her need to explore.

Pippa saw relationships in terms of chains to bind her to one path, one man, one life. He had to show her that together they could reach farther than they could apart. Today his campaign began. He would play to win because it was the only way he knew.

Pippa studied the sea lapping gently at the beach. The rhythm was calming, peaceful, so at odds with the morning and most of the afternoon she had spent with Josh. She sighed deeply and glanced at the sleeping man lying on the blanket beside her.

How he had the nerve to close his eyes in her presence was beyond her? Josh had done nothing but needle her all day. Spending hours poised halfway between laughter and murder, his, was not having a beneficial effect on her temper or her mood.

"Are you going to smolder for the rest of the afternoon?"

Josh looked at her through the shield of his lashes. So far, his plan had worked better than he had a right to expect. His woman was looking decidedly like a furious hornet hunting a place to sting. If the stakes hadn't been so high, he would have laughed at them both.

"I am not smoldering," she stated with awful calm. Her stare would have put a Borgia dagger to shame.

Josh rolled on his side, pillowing his head on his arm as he opened his eyes. "You're just angry because I wanted to poke around in all the places we could find."

"I almost ruined these shoes."

"I offered to buy you more suitable footwear," he pointed out. "Those little things are sexy as hell, but, as far as walking goes, they are a wipeout."

Pippa inhaled deeply, almost fooled into retaliation. But something about the look in his eyes damned the words on her tongue. She studied him intently.

He met her look, waiting.

The puzzle of his behavior, the tease, the quiet, the repartee that gave no quarter was suddenly clear. She could have kicked herself for letting her emotions cloud her thinking. Josh had made a point of keeping her off balance. That wasn't his style.

"What are you up to?" she asked in an altered tone. This time she would think before she felt.

"Wooing you," he replied promptly.

Whatever Pippa had expected it hadn't been this. Her mouth dropped open inelegantly, her eyes widening.

"You didn't see that one coming." Josh chuckled at her blank expression. "I wish I had a camera."

Her teeth closed with a snap. "You had better be glad that you don't. Of all the asinine things to say. What would you know about wooing? Let me tell you, even if I were in the market for a permanent man in my life, this is the wrong way to go about it."

Josh caught her hand, tumbling her against his chest before she could realize his intent. "Is it, woman of mine? I have your attention. In fact, I doubt there hast been a second today you haven't been watching me. I like that."

"Anyone watches a snake in paradise," she responded, trying without success to wriggle out of his hold. Her eyes narrowed. "I will give you about three seconds to let go of me."

"And then what?" he interrupted.

"I get even in a way you won't like. My roaming around has taught me quite a few tricks for discouraging, if not disabling, inopportune males."

He tipped his head, looking interested. Pippa glared.

He counted to three slowly. Pippa lifted her hand.

He lay there, watching her but making no move to protect himself.

"You haven't done anything," he murmured when three seconds became ten.

"Blast you, let me go," Pippa commanded, at the end of her emotional rope.

Josh shook his head, his eyes holding a kind of pity mixed with purpose. "No. I belong to you, and you belong to me. Before this trip is over, you're going to admit it."

"I will admit nothing except you are the most irritating, aggravating, sneaky, arrogant, low-dealing..." She paused only long enough to draw in a deep breath for the next tenth of the list." Rotten, manipulating..."

Josh closed her mouth by the simple method of covering her lips with his. Her grunts were hardly romantic, but a desperate man would take just about anything he could get.

Pippa struggled. He held on. Suddenly. she stopped, her breath a long moan of capitulation. He raised his head, staring into her eyes. The tears welling there almost hurt to see. If he hadn't been fighting for their future, he would have given up then. He touched her cheek, stroking the hot curve tenderly.

"It doesn't have to be like this. I love you. It doesn't have to be a battle for supremacy. I want to give to you, not take. But I will not let you walk away. You said that you loved me. Can you take that back?"

"With every breath that I draw I wish I could," she stated half in defiance and half in despair.

He closed his eyes on the pain of her admission, then looked at her silently.

Pippa stared back, seeing the courage he had and she didn't. "I can't, Josh."

He waited.

"You're asking me to change."

"Am I, Pippa? Or is it you who is demanding you change? If I had wanted what you think I do, I would have stayed in Jacksonville with Lisa. I want you as you are. Not altered to some mythical image you think I have of you."

Every nerve screamed a silent no. Pippa tensed, fighting the truth and the tomorrows he held before her as gold for a beggar.

"I want you in my life. I am prepared to share with you as l have never shared with anyone else. I don't trust easily either and yet I trust you. A moment ago, you could have hurt me. I knew you weren't bluffing."

The tears slipped down her face, leaving silver tracks to mark their passage. He was beginning to understand her, perhaps in places better than she understood herself. All her life, she hadn't fit with anyone, had given up hope of ever finding one person to accept her on her own terms. Josh was offering her the dream she had given up.

"It's too late," she whispered. "I'm not twenty anymore."

He shook his head, loving her enough to believe. "Only if you wish it to be too late. I'm here and so are you. We can do anything together."

Pippa pushed at his arms.

This time he let her go. His eyes followed her as she moved to the far corner of the blanket to stare out to sea.

"I have to think. I've been so positive that being alone was the only life I could expect. I don't know if I want to change now."

"Has it occurred to you that you are already changing, or you wouldn't even be listening to me?"

She turned her head, her lips curved into a faint, sad smile. "It had occurred to me. I would rather it hadn't to you, however."

He rolled into a sitting position. "I didn't know I could feel what another person was feeling. I'm no more accustomed to this emotion between us than you."

"We both could be wrong. It could be a middle age aberration."

He gave her a straight look which she deflected with a shrug. "I may be off balance with what's happening, but I am not that far off course. I don't think you are, either. How have you been sleeping?"

There was no point in lying. "Miserably."

"Same here. Pippa, I want to go forward to what could be."

Pippa spread her hands, for the first time in her life unable to make a decision. "I can't think, Josh. I don't know what I want or what I don't want. I need time, and that sounds like a virgin's excuse."

Josh took her hands in his. "As long as you are giving us the time, then you can have what you need. I have waited this long. I can wait if that's what it takes."

She looked into his eyes, fighting the urge to say yes right then. It would be so easy. But if she came to him, her doubts had to be gone. For if she took his name and committed her life, there was no going back. Her decision would be forever and a year.

"We have the time," she said finally. Denial hadn't worked. Lying to herself wasn't an option now. All or nothing.

CHAPTER
SEVENTEEN

"That was a fabulous dinner," Pippa murmured, leaning her head against Josh's shoulder.

Lyla walked beside her; her arm linked with Joe's. "I don't think I have ever had such wonderful duck in my life," Lyla added, sighing softly.

Josh looked at Joe over the women's heads. "I didn't know feeding them well would have such a good effect."

Joe chuckled, hugging Lyla close. "I'll have to remember this for future reference after we're married."

Lyla pouted up at him. "You promised you wouldn't rush me."

"Married!" Josh and Pippa said simultaneously.

"When did this happen?" Pippa asked, beating Josh to the question.

"It hasn't yet. I'm just working on her arguments. She has some stupid idea that her past will be a stumbling block. I don't intend to let her get away with that kind of cop-out."

The four stopped, the older couple studying the younger. Lyla focused on Pippa's face, feeling if she won her over, Josh would follow.

"I'm not brave enough to spend the rest of my life without Joe, but I thought if we waited it wouldn't be so bad. Once the press and this second trial is over, maybe people will forget about me and I can get on with my life."

"So, what are you going to do? Sit around for who knows how long while this wonderful, mythical timetable is set in motion?" Pippa demanded bluntly. "It could take years."

Josh watched his brother, sympathizing with his situation. When a man finally committed himself to a woman, waiting was the last thing on his mind.

"Let the fools gape," he stated abruptly. "If Joe says he can handle the gossip, then that's all that matters."

Lyla stared at him, startled at the challenge. She had thought Josh would understand her reasoning. She had always felt that the only reason he was helping her was because of Pippa not because he actually believed in her innocence.

"I thought you would see my point. You certainly didn't want me anywhere near any of you in the beginning."

"No, I didn't," he admitted. He paused a moment to grin at Pippa's irritated expression.

"Take that fierce look off your face, my love. There is no sense in trying to pretend I didn't see Lyla the way you and Joe did. I'm not into lying any more than you are."

It was Joe's turn to gape. "Your love. Since when?"

Lyla gave him an unladylike poke in the ribs. "Be quiet. It's none of our business."

"You could have been a little more subtle," Pippa muttered.

Josh laughed. "I'm trying to get her to make an honest man out of me, but she won't do it."

"Why?" Joe and Lyla asked together.

Pippa rolled her eyes. "This is where we came in." She yanked on Josh's arm. "I absolutely refuse to stand in front of a pink-and-white gingerbread house discussing my future. I feel like something out of Mother Goose."

"I'll second that," Lyla added, doing some pulling of her own.

"Do you suppose we should team up?" Joe asked Josh. "It looks as though we have the same problem."

"A load of female nonsense," Josh agreed.

Pippa stopped like a horse jibbing at a too high gate. "Of all the rotten..."

Before she could finish her assault on Josh's personality, Joe stiffened, his face changing.

"Damn." he swore angrily. "Josh, on your right!" he commanded abruptly, swinging to his left. "Lyla, Pippa, get to the car!"

Pippa whirled out of Josh's hold, grabbing Lyla's hand just as three men came out of the shadows of the trees surrounding the parking lot. Josh stepped into the path of one man as the sound of flesh connecting with flesh signaled the impact between Joe and the second. The third blocked Pippa and Lyla's way.

A flash of muted moonlight on a knife blade was all the warning Pippa had. Thrusting Lyla behind her, she crouched, her eyes slits of fury in a pale face. She hadn't exaggerated when she had told Josh she knew how to defend herself.

"So, you think you can take me on, little lady," the man crooned, eyeing her stance but clearly unimpressed.

Pippa didn't blink, didn't move. Her whole attention was trained on the man who would kill them if he could. All around her the sounds of Josh and Joe trying to protect her and Lyla filled her senses.

The man moved closer, and still Pippa waited. Her moment was coming. His eyes and weapon hand were the key. Suddenly the knife sliced forward.

Pippa feinted to the right, swinging her leg in a wide arc that caught the assailant just below the knees. He crashed over, rolling on his shoulder and coming up as swiftly as he had toppled. His face was twisted now, a mask of hate.

"Stupid move, beautiful." The murderous intent in his voice made the compliment an obscene parody. "You hurt me."

Again, Pippa said nothing. He was three times her size, armed and ready to kill. She had only the martial arts knowledge learned years ago and practiced daily to keep her and Lyla safe until Josh could come for her.

This time the man moved more cautiously, treating her with respect. He circled, his knife making testing darts at her body. Pippa dodged the ones coming too close. She watched and waited. Finally, tired of the game and hearing the beginning of the end of the battle behind him, he dove in for the kill.

Pippa bent low so that the knife whistled over her head. Her hand stiff, she used the power of her legs to drive her body upward as she jammed her palm into his chest, hearing the air whoosh from his lungs. He stumbled back from the force of her blow.

As he started to crumple, she slipped past him, using her other hand to deliver the final knockout punch. He fell like a downed tree at her feet. She stood braced for a moment to be sure that he was down and really out. Her sensei had drummed that lesson into her the first time she had taken him to the mat.

Down did not always mean out of action. When he didn't move, she slowly relaxed her battle stance. As she straightened, she turned to find Lyla staring at her as though she had never seen her before.

Josh was straddle-legged over his unconscious opponent and Joe was leaning against a palm with his man slumped, moaning on the ground at the base of the trunk.

Pippa looked away for a moment. The disbelief in Joe's expression and the horror in Lyla's licked at her temper. What had they expected? That she would let that creep get to Lyla?

She turned back, her eyes glittering with tears of fear that she hadn't allowed to paralyze her at the second she needed her wits the most. Frustration about how others saw her dried the moisture before it had a chance to leak from her eyes.

That odd woman! How many times had she heard that phrase? She hated the thought. She knew she was different, had always done what few women would dare.

She couldn't look at Josh as she bent to retrieve the handbag that she had dropped in the fight. She didn't want to see the same look in his eyes as that of Joe and Lyla.

When she straightened, Josh was there. He lifted her chin with his finger.

She sniffed, furious at herself for expecting more than the past had taught her existed.

"I hate crying. It's utterly useless and a total waste of time."

There was a bruise on the right side of his jaw and his hair had fallen over his forehead. His tie was askew and his jacket torn.

Pippa had never needed to lay her head on his shoulder more. Not because she couldn't stand on her own but because she was very glad they were all safe.

He touched her cheek, smiling. "Honey, I wish I'd had a camera. That last move was one beautiful piece of work. You not evened the odds for Joe and me but you saved Lyla's life."

She sniffed again, searching his face. His sincerity was almost impossible to believe. "We all did," she said finally.

He shook his head. "No, those two were supposed to keep Joe and me busy. That one was the danger. He figured two women alone would be a piece of cake. He didn't know my Pippa."

Pippa blinked in surprise. "You don't mind?"

"For having you and Lyla alive? Don't be a fool." He hauled her into his arms, his pride in her more than words could have expressed.

Pippa gulped, knowing that she was going to do something she had never done. "I am going to ruin your jacket," she whispered brokenly.

He leaned his chin on her hair, tucking her head against his heart. "You can ruin every piece of clothing I possess and turn yourself into a rainy-day panda with mascara running down your beautiful face and I would still love you."

The tears came then. She snuggled close, not even noticing when Lyla raced for the restaurant to call the police or that Joe stood watch over their attackers.

Josh was all that mattered and all she needed. When reality had come down to survival with no frills attached. she had fought for her life, aware that Josh was trying to reach her. Her faith had been in her man and herself.

His pride and faith in her had been all that she could have asked. He had not lied. He would not ask of her more than she could give. He knew her weak spots and didn't care. He loved her anyway. She raised her head, smile through her tears.

"When do you want to get married?"

Josh hugged her hard, tipped back his head, and laughed for the sheer joy of the moment. Then he kissed her hard.

"As soon as I can get the paperwork set and you can get your family in gear."

"We don't have to wait for them."

"They matter to you. I want them to share this with us."

She touched his cheek. "How can you know me so well?"

His eyes met hers. "I know you with every beat of my heart. I want you with every breath that I draw, and I think of you at every moment. There is no way I cannot know you."

"I love you."

"That's all I ask."

EPILOGUE

"Josh, slow down," Pippa gasped, rolling with the contractions threatening to rip her body in two. Labor was not for the faint of heart.

Josh slanted her look. "How far apart are the pains?" he demanded.

"Three minutes." She grinned at his succinct oath. "Well, how was I to know that labor for a woman my age could go this fast?"

He growled something unprintable, and Pippa laughed. She curled her arms about the mound of her stomach, feeling so happy she could have hugged the world.

Josh, her marriage, and now labor and delivery. This past year had given her so much that nothing could mar her delight. What were a few pains in comparison to the rewards?

"I don't believe I let you talk me into this," he muttered, taking a corner on two wheels.

Pippa giggled, and he glared at her.

"I still think that quack doctor lied. Forty-two-year-old women should not have to go through giving birth. Hell, forty-eight-year-old men shouldn't be looking at fatherhood for the first time."

He sent the car racing up the ramp to the emergency room entrance, slamming on the brakes. Pippa remembered Josh's joy at her news of her pregnancy. It was only his concern for her and his need to do something, anything to help when there was little, he could do that made him say words with no truth.

Before she could reassure him that everything was well in hand, Josh was around the car and helping her out. At that moment, another pain gripped her. She bent, trying to remember the breathing pattern she and Josh had learned in childbirth classes.

His arms were there, supporting her as they had all along. His voice reached through the pain, soothing her tense muscles, repeating the drill so that she suddenly was with him as they rode the wave of the contraction. When it was over, he lifted her in his arms and carried her through the doors.

"Not another word about being able to walk yourself," he decreed before shouting for a nurse. "This is my wife, Pippa Luck. She's having a baby," he stated urgently as a uniformed volunteer reached him.

The auxiliary woman pushed a wheelchair. "What are you doing down here again? We've already sent you upstairs. Did you get lost?"

Josh froze with Pippa in his arms. "Lady, l have not been anywhere near this hospital today. What are you talking about?"

The woman peered at Pippa and backed up hurriedly. "But I was so sure. You're blonde."

Of course, she is blonde. She's the only wife I have." The desk nurse joined them, frowning at the raised voices. "Sir, I must ask you to be quiet." She glanced at Pippa. "You are...?"

"Mrs. Joshua Luck."

The nurse frowned. "But I thought you already went upstairs."

"That's what I was trying to tell this man," the auxiliary put in helpfully. "I know her doctor is waiting for her."

"Well, how did they get back down here?"

"I don't believe this," Josh roared, looking harassed.

Pippa struggled not to laugh through the increasing tightness in her lower body. Josh and Joe had become so much closer in the last year, often being in the same place at the same time. Their marked resemblance had caused a lot of confusion at first. Both men had found the situation annoying.

She and Lyla had shared so much fun watching the two cope with the situation. Today was not a good moment for Josh to handle the close resemblance. More importantly, she didn't have the time. She tugged on his ear.

He glared down at her.

"I think just maybe Lyla and Joe have beat us to the hospital," she murmured.

If anything, Josh looked more irritated, not less.

"I don't care if my brother has ten kids. He may not do so at your expense."

"You have a brother with a wife delivering today?" the nurse asked.

Josh focused on her. "How the devil do I know? All I know is that if we don't get moving, my wife is going to give birth in this damn hall and I'm going to own this hospital. Her pains are less than three minutes apart."

As if to prove his point, another contraction swelled. Josh swore, and the emergency room personnel moved swiftly. In moments, Pippa was on her way upstairs with Josh's hand wrapped securely around her own. His voice and touch were with her through every step in the process.

It was his shoulder on which she laid her head when the doctor decided that her labor was slowing and that a Cesarean would be necessary. Josh's kiss was on her lips as she closed her eyes and let the anesthetic take her away.

"I wish you would stop pacing. You're not helping Pippa or me. Try being calm," Joe muttered, glaring at his brother.

Since Joe was marking the length of the waiting room going in the opposite direction, the remark was singularly ill advised. Josh slanted him a look that spoke volumes.

"I would like to know the odds of Lyla and Pippa delivering on the same day and having almost the same problem."

Joe shrugged, glancing at the door through which the doctor or nurse would be coming to give them the news.

"How would I know? Genetics. You and I are big men and both Lyla and Pippa are delicately made. The thing I can't get over was that Lyla didn't tell me a Cesarean was a possibility."

Josh scowled. "Yeah, same here. As soon as Pippa is back on her feet, her tail feathers are going to be damn sore. Of all the dumb stunts. I love that woman to distraction, but sometimes she could drive a saint to mayhem. What do I know about kids at my age? We have you and Lyla making babies. Why do we have to?"

Joe stopped, staring at his brother. "I thought you wanted this child."

"Not at Pippa's expense I don't," he returned baldly, letting his fear show for the first time.

"Pippa wanting to do natural childbirth was enough of a shock to my system. Those classes the four of us attended were mind boggling. I had no idea. Now this C-section thing. It isn't the same."

Joe came to him, just as worried as his brother but knowing he had no reason to be. His future with Lyla was clear and bright. With the death by a heart attack of Navaro three months ago, the last blot on their horizon had been lifted.

Before the morning was over, Lyla would give birth to a beautiful little girl with her mother's dark eyes and his mother's dark red hair.

They would name her Joy. He touched Josh's shoulder, unsurprised at the rock-hard feel of his muscles.

"Pippa will be fine," he murmured, looking into his brother's future. His gift would be welcomed, he knew, and he gave it with love.

Josh searched Joe's eyes. He no longer had to fight to accept his brother and his power. "You're sure?"

"Very sure."

Josh nodded then sighed deeply. "Do you know the sex of the baby? Right now, I'm wishing that I hadn't agreed with Pippa that we wanted it to be a surprise."

Joe grinned, holding Pippa's wish safe. "Yes, but I'm not going to tell you. Some things are better as surprises."

As long as Pippa was all right, Josh didn't really care about the rest, but he continued the conversation to pass the time. Anything was better than watching the clock tick too slowly to the next minute.

"Mr. Luck?"

Both men turned to the nurse standing in the doorway. Joe chuckled softly. "This one is for you, big brother."

"You have a six-pound-eight-ounce boy."

Josh started to move. Joe stopped him with a hand on his shoulder. "Wait."

Josh's brows rose.

The nurse completed her news. "And a five pound-ten-ounce girl."

Josh looked at Joe's face as the news sank in. For a long moment he couldn't think of the words to describe his feelings. Two babies? The doctor would have told Pippa. The little witch had sworn the man to secrecy. He knew she had seemed bigger than Lyla. He hardly recognized his own voice when he finally found the words to express his feelings.

"I'll kill her," he said faintly, his face pale. "No jury in the state will convict me. That woman had to have known about this. She even coerced that damn quack into keeping quiet. And I pay his bills, damn him. A father has rights too."

Joe roared with laughter, knowing that Josh would take one look at his pale-eyed wife and cave in. Pippa had that kind of way about her. In less than twenty-four hours, if that long, Pippa would have Josh convinced that two children were just as easy to raise as one. After all, they weren't getting any younger.

What good would it have done to tell him about something that would only worry him. It all had come out perfectly in the end.

Smiling to himself, Joe started measuring the floor again. After all, it was tradition for a man, even one who knew the future to pace, he reminded himself.

Josh glared at his brother's grin. He thought his wife's plan was funny, did he? Revenge was honey sweet and he knew just how to serve it.

"You know, Pippa loves matching people up. I wonder who she'll decide will do for your children since you and Lyla are planning on more than one. Think of the possibilities."

Joe stopped in midstride, his own face paling. "She wouldn't," he gulped, knowing very well

Pippa was capable of anything when the mood struck. She could give lessons to the military on strategy and planning. Her creativity was already legendary among their mutual friends.

Thank God she had chosen Josh and not him. Living with that stick of female explosive would have destroyed his peace forever.

Josh watched his retribution sink in. If he had to suffer, the least Joe could do was suffer with him. "Want to bet?" he asked with a grin, enjoying the images his future held.

Pippa was sure to make him crazy for the rest of their life together but he wouldn't have it any other way. But no more delivery room surprises. That was so not ever happening again.

Two babies! Trust Pippa to find a way to talk him into not having an only child. Maybe he wouldn't need that trial by jury after all.

ABOUT THE
AUTHOR

Why would a traditionally published author, published internationally with over thirty books in more than twenty languages and two lifetime achievement awards just to name few accolades, choose to self-publish?

If your first answer is that she has lost her mind, my answer is NO!

You'll notice the capital letters. Film stars regularly finance and produce their movies and movies of other stars. Why can't authors choose to produce their books, leaving behind the traditional format for the freedom of writing what the author wants and when the author wants to write?

I haven't lost my mind. I've gained by creative freedom. Writing is more than a career for me. It always has been, from the moment I ran out of books and decided, for my sanity's sake, to write a story while I waited for more books to arrive. A fluke involving another writer who had just started a writing club was my first brush with the machinery that is traditional publishing.

LACEY DANCER

It was supposed to be hard to get an agent. That writer thought I had talent, although she didn't tell me that at the time, and she sent my story to her agent. I sold four books that year.

I discovered that interesting word genre. Darn it. I had to write a certain way. Because I had a 'male' name and only women wrote romances at that time, I had to have a pen name. Because I wrote faster than my home house would publish a single writer, my agent sent my extra stories to other houses. Each wanted a different pen name. Hence, I have multiple pen names.

Lacey Dancer was and is my favorite. It represents a moment in my life when I called a halt to the process of traditional publishing. I was worn out by the rules and requirements. I understood their business model and it does work for publishing in general. It didn't work for me the writer. I wanted to create real people characters, dealing with real problems. Life is too interesting to be reduced to a fairy tale.

After a discussion with my agent, I decided to quit. I wasn't the first to make that decision. She had four of my books at the time, another Series that I knew none of houses for which I worked would even consider because one of the main characters was too old to fit the profile of what they believed sold.

Unknown to me, she sent those books to a new house, one which didn't have a profile or requirements. The house bought all four books. I loved working for Meteor and Kismet Publishing. The character that no one would have considered was very popular. Her name was Pippa and her author is Lacey Dancer.

When Meteor was sold to its biggest competitor, I decided for family reasons to retire from writing. I missed writing too much to stay retired. Computers, the internet and social media arrived and opened doors to new ideas and ways to publish.

I love a challenge and I really like breaking new ground. Is it easy? Absolutely not. There are more questions than answers some days.

For me, this new world of publishing is tailor made. I make my own rules, write my way, stories I like with characters that drive me nuts on a good day and make me crazy on a busy day. I love what I do. I especially love the freedom of doing what I do my way.

CONTACT THE AUTHOR

International, Award-Winning Romance and Suspense author, Sydney Clary a.k.a. Lacey Dancer, has written and published over 36 books over her lifetime that have been published in 20 different languages in over 100 countries. She is working on adding 20 or 30 more to the count as well as bringing her backlist into the 21st century. During her writing career she has garnered 2 Lifetime Achievement awards from the Romance Writers of America.

Email: laceydancerauthor@gmail.com
Website: https://laceydancer.com
Twitter: https://twitter.com/LaceyTheAuthor
Instagram: https://www.instagram.com/laceydancerauthor/
Facebook: https://www.facebook.com/BooksByLaceyDancer/
LinkedIn: https://www.linkedin.com/in/Lacey-Dancer-Author
YouTube: https://www.youtube.com/@laceydancerauthor
Pinterest: https://www.pinterest.com/laceydancerauthor/
Goodreads: https://www.goodreads.com/author/show/362798.Lacey_Dancer

OTHER BOOKS BY THIS AUTHOR

The Live Oak Series

Live Oak is a real place. Small towns all over the country are struggling to keep their way of life and heritage intact and still survive in the 21st century. That is the background for the Live Oak Series, but the characters are the heart of the stories, their struggles, triumphs, and solutions to the twists and turns in life. Live Oak in my fictional world is filled with challenges and triumphs.

Every character in this series is fictional. Except two. Those two are Jennifer and Tina who appear in books three and four. These two friends of mine talked me into putting them in the story. We made a deal. Each had to create her own physical description. Each will have her own book. I am working on Jennifer's now.

A stalker sneaks into town to kill. Country justice comes in the form of an irate donkey named Jay.

A city woman who needs her lattes and shoe stores discovers the misadventures of tractors and barnyard animals that have no idea when to shut up in the morning. Normal people do not wake up at dawn.

The construction crew arrives to build a vision of the future for Live Oak. Mother Nature has other ideas with a hurricane on the east coast and a bomb on the west coast.

Add in a child escaping terrible abuse and neglect, a cranky judge, a sheriff who heads the local country band, and a wounded veteran who is not going to give up and the plot thickens with every book.

That doesn't count the three weddings to date and two more in the future.

Chase the Fire[1] - Book 1
Playing with Fire[2] - Book 2
Strike the Fire[3] - Book 3
Catch the Fire[4] - Book 4
Light the Fire[5] - Book 5

---

1. https://books2read.com/ChaseTheFireBook1

2. https://books2read.com/PlayingWithFireBook2

3. https://books2read.com/StrikeTheFireBook3

4. https://books2read.com/CatchTheFireBook4

5. https://books2read.com/Light-The-Fire-Book-5

The Pippa Series

Pippa, an aunt, a friend, a writer. Following rules, unless they are her own, is so not on her agenda. She writes and values her solitude. Birthdays, specifically hers, are not to be celebrated. Have a permanent man in her life is a complication she can happily forgo. However, her relatives and friends might just need a little help in finding a life partner. And she loves a challenge.

Tragically injured, hiding from the world, her niece. Lorelei is the first to discover how ingenious a loving, determined woman can be. Pippa issues a challenge. The doctors are positive Lorelei will never walk again. Pippa dares Lorelei to prove them wrong. *"Come live with me and rebuild your life. Needing a place to recover, Lorelei accepts the challenge."*

When a workaholic male appears in the neighborhood, Pippa takes his measure and makes her plans. The impossible becomes very possible.

Pippa decides that her plans worked so well with Lorelei, she really must do something about her nephew, Jason. The Iceman faces the frozen wasteland of his life as Pippa adroitly maneuvers him into meeting Diana Diamond. Diana shuns the spotlight and Jason lives for it. Opposites are so much fun to match, especially as the sparks fly. Yes, she definitely has her hands full with these two but she is up for the challenge.

With two successes to her personal credit, Pippa decides on a trip, a thirteen-day cruise. Wow, Lilah is like a wounded creature, hiding from the media, shrinking from the least contact. Pippa reaches out even as she is discovering her own match in Joshua Luck.

Joshua is stunned at the woman who challenges and entices with every word, every move. Following her thought processes is like chasing a rabbit on steroids. Pippa is like no woman he has ever met. She makes her own rules, delves into lives, meddling, and arranging with such heart it is impossible not to admire her tactics even as he deals with his reaction to her.

She makes the rules, breaks the rules, and dares everyone with whom she comes in contact to reach for their every wish and dream. The bigger the challenge, the happier Pippa is. Impossible is a word she doesn't recognize, and no is a word she ignores.

What's a man to do with a woman like that? Marry her? Spend his life wondering what she will do next? Who will she decide needs her special matchmaking touch?

Choices[6] – Book 1

Diamonds and Ice[7] – Book 2

Thirteen Nights of Luck[8] – Book 3

---

6. https://books2read.com/ChoicesBook1

7. https://books2read.com/DiamondAndIceBook2

8. https://books2read.com/ThirteenNightsOfLuckBook3

The Truth Series

Felicity Ramsey could be anyone. Your best friend? Your worst enemy? She moved through the shadows without making a sound, no warning given. She was a hunter. She had been taught from the cradle how to seek her prey and make the kill. She hated killing but she killed. Her prey was the monster who could escape the law, could hide in plain sight from justice.

Evidence and alibis could be manufactured. Governmental lines could become borders over which the law could not pass. The monsters were many. She was just one. But there were more. The human weapons trained and formed by governments to fight wars with no real winners. Men and women who could not forget the lethal skills they had learned and reenter the world that they had fought to protect.

Skye Farm and Skye/Sea were born, created on her own private mountain. The Farm was home and haven to those lost warriors who no longer had a place in civilization. Their skills and training were sought and valued by the government and the private sector.

Secure on her mountain, Felicity sought the monsters the law could not catch or exact retribution. She worked alone until one man; Ace Faulkner faced her in a room with a friend beaten to near death lying on the floor between them.

Ace had a choice. Shoot to kill? Or holster his gun?

Felicity had a choice. Trust the man? Or save the woman at her feet?

One choice made. Two guns laid aside to save a life.

Two loners, working together.

An expected phone call on a line that no one should have, creates a threat to everything that Felicity has built, the Farm, the Ranch and all those who work and live on her three mountains. A code 'blue' thrown over all of Skye/Sea. An infiltration by foreign interests in Washington, an accidental death of a loved one of one of their own has created more questions rather than answers.

In the air, on the sea and on the land, the teams gear up to protect their home and find the traitors in their government who profited from their acts of treason.

Truth Kills[9] – Book 1

Truth Tells[10] – Book 2

Truth Wins[11] – Book 3

BOOK BY SYDNEY CLARY

Are you facing the task of care for an aging relative, a child or loved one through a serious illness? This book is a real-life approach to handling the multitude of problems that crop up each day.

In your home, in a care facility and all the variations of caregiving locations, there are ways to help those who matter to you and help yourself survive the stress and strain of caregiving.

- How to wait in waiting rooms.
- How to find a new location for your loved one when the present situation no longer meets the needs of your relative or friend.
- How to handle medical insurance.
- How to handle home care.
- How to resolve problems with medical staff.
- How to get bills paid.

There are answers to these issues and many others, real-life answers that work. Need an idea or new avenue for that dead-end you are facing as a caregiver.

The goal of this book is to provide those answers, those suggestions. Examples of use are in every chapter, real people dealing with problems and solutions. Some will make you smile; some will make you cry but each will show what can be done as you face this demanding and rewarding task in your own life.

Caregiving: Real Life Answers[1]

---

1.   https://books2read.com/CareGivingByClary

BACK BOOK LISTING
FOR LACEY DANCER

Only available at used paperback book outlets*(enhanced and revised)
Single novel
   Sunlight on Shadows (1991)
   Baby Makes Five (1992)
Starke-McGuire
   Silent Enchantment (1990) – Re-released and enhanced titled – Choices*
   Diamond On Ice (1991) – Re-released and enhanced titled – Diamond and Ice*
   13 Days of Luck (1991) – Re-released and enhanced titled – Thirteen Nights of Luck*
   Flight of the Swan (1992)
   Forever Joy (1993)
   Lightning Strikes Twice (1993)
   His Woman's Gift (1993)
   Many Faces of Love (2003)
St. James Series
   Silke (1996)
   Caprice (1996)
   Leora (1996)
   Noelle (1996)